T0132449

Questings: A Parable

Jonathan Bryan

iUniverse, Inc.
New York   Bloomington

iUniverse books may be ordered through booksellers or by contacting:

iUniverse
1663 Liberty Drive
Bloomington, IN 47403
www.iuniverse.com
1-800-Authors (1-800-288-4677)

ISBN: 978-1-4401-6348-7 (sc)
ISBN: 978-1-4401-6349-4 (ebook)

Printed in the United States of America

iUniverse rev. date: 09/24/2009

Also by Jonathan Bryan

A Life of Love, A Love of Life: Recollections of Our Family (coauthored with Alice Bryan Juhan and Mary Bryan Fuller), 2002.

CrossRoads: Musings on a Father-Son Pilgrimage (coauthored with Alex Bryan), 2003.

Nonetheless, God Retrieves Us: What a Yellow Lab Taught Me about Retrieval Spirituality, 2006.

For Judy, Alex, Tucker, Mark, Kharis, Jordan, Bryan, Molly, Joey

Contents

Acknowledgments

Thanks to my students during these fifty years of teaching who have made me think and learn.

And thanks to the following who have given me insights for this book . . .

Ann Jackson, MBA, retired director of the Oregon Hospice Association and diagnosed with scleroderma in 2000, who clarified end-of-life issues around advance directives, patients' rights, and hospice care. http://oregonhospice.org and/or National Hospice and Palliative Care Organization at http://nhpco.org

Those who work on behalf of people struggling with scleroderma; with special thanks to the Scleroderma Foundation. http://www.scleroderma.org

The Charter for Compassion, led by Karen Armstrong, for their "collaborative effort to build a peaceful and harmonious global community" with the core belief "that while all faiths are not the same, they all share the core principle of compassion and the Golden Rule;" and "that the voice of negativity and violence so often associated with religion is the minority and that the voice of compassion is the majority." http://charterforcompassion.com

The BioLogos Foundation, led by Francis Collins, which "promotes the search for truth in both the natural and spiritual realms seeking harmony between these different perspectives," [since] "faith and science both lead to truth about God and creation." http://biologos.org

The Templeton Foundation, for serving as a "philanthropic catalyst for research and discoveries relating to what scientists and philosophers call the Big Questions," supporting "work at the world's top universities in such fields as theoretical physics, cosmology, evolutionary biology, cognitive science, and social science relating to love, forgiveness, creativity, purpose, and the nature and origin of religious belief." http://www.templeton.org

The National Center for Science Education (NCSE), for its dedication as a "not-for-profit, membership organization providing information and resources for schools, parents and concerned citizens working to keep evolution in public school science education." http://ncseweb.org/religion

Warren Muir, Executive Director, Division on Earth and Life Sciences of the National Academy of Sciences, which serves as "an honorific society of distinguished scholars engaged in scientific and engineering research, dedicated to the furtherance of science and technology and to their use for the general welfare" and for working to protect science education from religious encroachment: "The pressure to downplay evolution or emphasize nonscientific alternatives in public schools compromises science education. Despite the lack of scientific evidence for creationist positions, some advocates continue to demand that various forms of creationism be taught together with or in place of evolution in science classes." http://nationalacademies.org/evolution/ScienceAndReligion.html

The Clergy Letter Project, led by Michael Zimmerman, for collecting signatures of clerics who endorse this statement: "We the undersigned, Christian clergy from many different traditions, believe that the theory of evolution is a foundational scientific truth, one that has stood up to rigorous scrutiny and upon which much of human knowledge and achievement rests." http://www.butler.edu/clergyproject/rel_evol_sun.htm

1 A Peaceful Beginning

At dawn on this Saturday morning in the spring of 1954, I'm standing on the shoreline of a sheltered inlet called Misty Cove. It's on the Virginia side of the Potomac River just south of Alexandria.

The rising sun backlights Nomanisan Island, a couple of low-lying acres covered with tall trees and lush undergrowth. I notice a tarpaper shack on a rise of higher ground. A front porch, screened, some rough chairs, one window on the cove side, and a stone chimney in back. Nearby: a stone grill, an outhouse, a hammock between two trees, fishnets draped over some branches, old stars and stripes on a stripped-sapling pole, clothes on a clothesline. A short dock. Tied to it, a wooden skiff with an outboard on the transom. A rough footbridge spanning the narrow tidal gut separating the island from the main shoreline.

The sun's rays catch marsh grasses and cattails, dogwoods budding, an eagle soaring, gulls swooping, a blue heron winging, a fish breaking, a beaver paddling. An osprey diving. Egrets roosting. Squirrels scampering. Songs of redwing blackbirds, croaks of bullfrogs, caws of crows. A south breeze ripples the surface of Misty Cove. Peaceful. Ecological.

* * * * *

Later that morning, up the hill from Misty Cove in an upmarket neighborhood called Bon Vivant, a young family worked together in their back yard.

Hal, Sibyl, and little Frank Grant were building a new mast for their sailboat, laying long wooden strips into a laminate, securing them with marine glue, stainless screws, and temporary c-clamps. By sunset they had finished a pole twenty-six feet long. Sibyl nudged her husband, "Say, Prince Hal," she said in a lilting English accent, "I thought you were going to get these strips in white cedar. This looks like spruce." "It is," said Hal. "They were out of everything else."

The next morning Hal and Sibyl let young Frank take off the clamps while they admired the tight joints. Then they set to work with drawknife, plane, rasp, and sandpaper to shape their masterpiece. In mid-afternoon they applied the first marine varnish to clad the lamination against the weather. On Monday, while Hal was at work and Frank in school, Sibyl gave it the second coat, and on Tuesday the last. On Saturday the three Grants installed the rigging, stepped the new mast, and launched their nineteen-foot day sailer called Windermere into Misty Cove. They took their first sail of 1954.

* * * * *

At about the same time, many miles west, up in the Blue Ridge mountains of Virginia, at a certain rock outcropping, a short, muscled, red-haired young man stared up a cliff to the first big ledge. He stretched his arms wide, took a deep breath, reached high to get two handholds, lifted his right foot onto a foothold, and ascended.

In several more moves he climbed up and up, calm and deliberate. He stretched his right arm to a handhold in a crevice. He heard the rattle. He jerked his hand back. The rattler struck. It missed. His right foot slipped. Only one hand and one foot connected him to the rock face. They slipped.

* * * * *

Well, that's three little clips to get us going. The story flowing from these raises questions that I hope you will want to engage:

How do things happen? By what mechanisms? Why do things happen? For what purposes? What meanings? Who or what runs this universe, anyhow? Why so much conflict? And suffering? Why such disputes between Christian fundamentalists and scientific fundamentalists? How does reconciliation work?

Many other questions will emerge, but those will serve as starters.

Nomanisan Island? John Donne (1572-1631), dean of St. Paul's Cathedral, London, wrote an essay, "Meditation 16," published in *Devotions Upon Emergent Occasions* (1624) using the phrase "no man is an island unto himself."

* * * * *

On a warm afternoon in the following autumn a wooden skiff headed from Nomanisan Island toward the sailboat, the rower a boy, an older girl in the stern. He made good time, with strong strokes. He said, "I'm going sailing." She said, "Frank, you can't do that, you're only nine. Your father said you couldn't take the boat till you're thirteen." He laughed. "Lilly-Belle, I can sail better than you can." So Lilly-Belle decided to go along, because when you're almost twelve you must take care of the younger children. Her mother always told her, "We are entrusted to one another," and she believed her mother.

With lots of laughs they got the mainsail and jib up, cast off from the mooring, took the wind, and, Frank at the helm, set a course out of the cove into the river. They trimmed the sails close-hauled, their weight on the windward side balancing against gusts, shrouds and mainstay supporting the shiny-varnished mast, centerboard redirecting sideslip, tiller trimming the rudder. All forces compensated to equilibrium: canvas, bodies, weight, mass, wood, wind, and water.

An hour later the kids sailed back into the cove, playing with the boat, heeling and tacking and jibing and pirouetting to the melody of their laughter. They made one last flying jibe which caught the full force of the wind from behind and slapped the boom through an arc of a hundred and fifty degrees, fetching it up against the mainsheet at one end and the gooseneck at the other, torquing the mast. A hairline delamination opened. The eagle flew. From a hole under a sycamore a snake slid into the water.

The kids got Windermere moored and tidied up as they'd found it. Lilly-Belle rowed the skiff to the shore to let Frank off, then to Nomanisan Island to take her copy of *Huckleberry Finn* into the hammock to read all about the Mississippi and Huck and "sivilization." "'All right,' said Huck, 'I'll go to hell.'"

Frank walked up the hill to his big brick house. Sibyl greeted him with a hug and sent him up to get clean for supper. When Hal got home they ate together at the mahogany table.

Later that night a cold front arrived. In the morning, young Frank, chilly in the breeze from his window, woke up and watched the sun rise over the river, rays sparkling on the first dew on the last morning glories of that autumn.

* * * * *

The next morning Nonchalance McFinn walked with Lilly-Belle from the island to the school bus stop, saw her aboard, continued on to her garden, worked for three hours, and walked home past Bon Vivant with its well-built older homes set on generous, well-tended plots, down to the parkway, onto the dirt track leading to Misty Cove and the footbridge, crossed to Nomanisan Island, passed the fish-bake grill with its little hand-painted sign saying "Shadrach," entered her fine residence with its sign saying "Meshach," and lay down to rest. She chuckled as she thought of Nick bidding her climb in beside him, saying "Abedwego!" And the sign over the bed: "Fiery Furnace."

* * * * *

If you have gotten this far, you may welcome some preview. My parable follows Frank's life well into his middle age. That takes about half the pages. In the second half we reflect on the meaning of his life. Several characters, including Frank himself, offer their observations on what he has done and what has happened to him. And to them, and what it all means.

That part of the book lets me make certain points about life, spirituality, questing, why things happen, the Bible, theology, the origin of the universe, evolution, creationism, public policy, and other matters important to me. I hope also to you. That's why I call this a parable, for I intend it to carry meaning far beyond itself.

You could read the first half of the book as a sort of short novel and let it go at that. Or skip it and read the second half to find out what I think about all those vexing topics. Or even the whole book.

* * * * *

A few months later, in the spring of 1955, Frank, eager to launch Windermere, woke up early, leapt into his clothes, leapt onto the porch roof, leapt off the low side into the periwinkle, rolled down the incline, laughing, leapt onto his bike, sped toward his riverside. He flew down the dirt track, skidded to a sand-pitching stop on the beach, leapt from his bike. And his heart leapt up as he beheld the river, Misty Cove, Nomanisan Island, Windermere, all the constants of his life, the balance points of his child's serenity.

He watched surface mist rise from colder water to warmer air. Over the mist he saw only the island's treetops. He saw mist swirl as a breeze curled around the near shore waters. High up on the beach, well beyond the high-tide berm, Windermere sat where they had hauled her in late autumn, resting on her chocks. Frank shinnied onto the foredeck and watched the sun burn off the mist. He watched the eagle lift off from the sycamore tree, swoop to snatch a fish from the Cove, return to its limb.

Around eight-thirty, Sibyl and Hal showed up, Sibyl with a jug of hot chocolate, three mugs, and some brown bread. "Breakfast, maties!" They sat on a driftwood log, munching and sipping for a few quiet minutes until Hal said, "Let's go." Frank went to the boat shed and retrieved paint and gear. After a while he got to do what he loved: he varnished the mast and boom.

On the next Saturday morning, Windermere went into the cove and got her shakedown cruise, her gleeful crew eating and drinking, enjoying their river, their springtime life, their equinoctial moment, their boat, their threesome, laughing as Sibyl, pleasingly plump in a wholesome English sort of way, and Hal, downright portly, moved their considerable ballast where needed.

* * * * *

All through the 1950s, Nonchalance McFinn and Nick Spooner continued the routine they had established when they got together in early 1942 and had Lilly-Belle nine months later.

Nick sometimes caught some shad to bake on Shadrach, sometimes he caught a cold, sometimes he caught up on his sleep, always he caught up with his friends at Everybody's Inn. With no cash except his allowance from Nonnie, he stayed pretty sober, cadging cigarettes and "just a sip" from his friends. On Saturday nights he and the friends gathered at Buddy Simpson's double wide for poker so he could lose anything he had left.

On weekdays, Nonnie got Lilly-Belle off to school, worked her garden and orchard, or canned her harvest, or rowed her skiff out to empty her fish nets and pull her eel pots, or smoke her shad and eels. On rainy days she wrote her column for the Gazette or sewed her quilts or did the tailoring that housewives brought her from up the hill.

On Saturday mornings, soon after midnight, she started baking fresh bread and rolls for market. Well before dawn she made Nick get up to help her load the big skiff with all her foodstuff, hand-work, and other wares. Before first light she fired up the five horsepower Johnson outboard and motored up the river to the farmer's market in Alexandria. Every week at closing time she filled a box with some unsold food and sent it off with her friend Benny the jail guard to take to the town's inmates. "Nobody cares about them. Give 'em a little boost."

In these years, from time to time, one of the housewives from fancy Bon Vivant would visit Nomanisan Island for tea and conversation and ask why she, the housewife, felt so unfulfilled and why Nonnie had so much liberty and self-reliance. Well, honey, Nonnie would say with deep kindness, it comes at a cost. This bed of roses has thorns. And Nonchalance McFinn would gently let the housewife know why she of course would feel unfulfilled if she didn't place highest value on rearing strong children in a stable family where love prevails. Do that well, Nonnie would say, and be fulfilled. If Nonnie saw this go down well, she would urge the young housewife to "use some of this free time you get from all your newfangled time-savers like dishwashers and clothes dryers and remember the world of hurt out there where still lots of good folks got nothing much but pain and poverty, and volunteer your service." "Why?," the housewife would say. "Because, honey, you got it made and that incurs an obligation."

Sometimes the housewives in their coffee klatches compared notes about their tea-talk visits and sometimes one would actually do what Nonnie said and be fulfilled.

Because after all, it's not every day they got to hear a woman over six feet tall in her mid-fifties, lean and hard with the look of Indian and African and Saxon all at once, a voice resonating folk wisdom, eyes and hands moving calm and strong, hair natural and long, generally in a mammoth single braid, sometimes piled up with an old turkey-leg bone stuck through it.

Over these years, Nonchalance grew from strength to strength, a tower of simple nobility, a beacon of sanity on her island with her little no 'count mate drifting alongside her seeming to bring her happiness without ever being anything noticeable. Make no wake, said Nick, and he was really good at it.

By 1959 Nick had attained four years of formal education, thirteen years of emotional maturity, seventeen years of fatherhood, eighteen years of matehood, and forty-two years of mortal life. Then one Saturday night he never came home. His poker buddies said Nick had left the game about midnight talking about how his horoscope said he could make a million in Las Vegas so he thought he'd just up and go there. The last they saw him he was walking the wrong way on Route One. Nonnie grieved, Lilly-Belle grieved, then they got over it.

* * * * *

During those growing-up years Hal and Sibyl and Frank would often take Windermere out in early morning and sail her whichever way was upwind. Frank's parents would say, "Always go out upwind, Frank, so you have an easy run downwind to get home," and Frank learned to respond to the litany, "And that's true in life as well. Tough things first, easy later." On a few memorable occasions the three took supper and sailed way down the river, never mind the wind or the tide, and anchored in a little inlet to spend the night, Frank stretched out on the foredeck sort of wrapped around the mast, Hal and Sibyl on the floorboards, all three slapping mosquitoes, laughing and naming the stars. Nobody knew what the real names were, but they made up ones they thought were very funny.

* * * * *

Lilly-Belle excelled throughout her schooling. When she graduated from high school in 1959, she had a full scholarship to Wellesley. A remarkable student, bright and driven, she met everyone's expectations. Since she did overloads and summer school, she graduated a year early, in 1962, with high honors in English and another scholarship, this time at the American University in D.C., to begin her Ph.D.

Also that spring Frank graduated from high school. He spent the summer doing odd jobs and spending his money at a Georgetown night spot that didn't check ages. In September he went down to the University of Virginia in Charlottesville to do engineering, like his father.

* * * * *

I have introduced two families: Hal, Sibyl, and Frank Grant; and Lilly-Belle and Nonchalance (Nonnie) McFinn; plus, briefly, Nick Spooner. And I have titled this chapter "A Peaceful Beginning." The obvious reason for this will become, as my parable goes on, far more complex and, I hope, interesting and significant.

2 Alienation in the Year from Hell

Emily and Brad Farrier lived in a solid 1920s three-story fieldstone house across the street from Hal and Sibyl Grant in Bon Vivant. Like the Grants, they could look down the hill to the country club, the golf course, and the Potomac. On Sunday morning, January 6, 1963, they faced each other across their antique table in their bay-windowed breakfast nook. Emily tasted her soft-boiled egg and said, "By the way, I'm having lunch with Sibyl today." Brad said, "Well, I'm playing tennis with Hal. At the club at one-thirty." "Oh, I'll still be there. Maybe see you." "Maybe. I hope so."

The sun, on this winter mid-morning, shot through the bare trees. Brad adjusted the blinds. Their maid, in starched uniform and cap, cleared their dishes and refilled their coffee cups. "Thank you, Edna." Emily reached across to take Brad's hand. "I read Eliot's 'Hollow Men' again. I feel hollow, Brad, stuffed with stuff, my head empty, like straw." Brad said, "Yesterday you said you felt like Prufrock, your life measured with coffee spoons. We have to do something about this." "Yes. It's all so empty. We've got everything. And nothing. When it happened . . . ." Brad looked into her elegant face. She looked down the hill and murmured, "All meaning died. Why can't we know why?" Silence.

Emily said, "You know the new neighbor, the red-haired guy? Sibyl told me that she talked to him. He's both a minister and a lawyer. She liked him." Emily sat back. "Brad, I want to talk to a minister." Brad said, "Yes. Maybe he could help."

When they got back from the club that afternoon, they walked over to the young minister's garage apartment and introduced themselves. "Nice to know you," he said. "I'm Phil Imbroglio." He invited them in. He told them about himself and listened as they told him about their meaningless life, their coffee-spoon lives, heads stuffed with straw. They told him about their lost cause, Brad's brother Stevie, serving a thirty-year term, estranged and refusing to speak. How come this calamity in Stevie's life? Why? And about Stevie's wife and children, bitter, reclusive, broken, and broke. They asked him why this happened, why it wouldn't resolve, why it bothered them constantly. They asked him why they felt so empty in all their prosperity, comfortable home, things, career, and social doings.

He named the problem: acedia, spiritual emptiness. Yes, the Farriers said. They discussed it for a while. The Farriers invited him for supper the next Sunday. Afterward, Emily said, "That worked for me." Brad said, "And for me." It began a long tradition of meals and conversations, frequently about why things happen, good things and bad things, and fulfillment despite despair.

* * * * *

Phil took a walk after supper. He encountered a woman who greeted him with a hearty "Hello, neighbor." Phil stopped and introduced himself. She had a strong smile, a worn wool plaid shirt, heavy trousers, mud-stained boots, a peasant scarf, and no makeup. She said, "I'm Nonchalance McFinn, the outsider." "Outside of what?" "This neighborhood. I live on Nomanisan Island, down in Misty Cove." Phil told a bit about himself. They chatted. They agreed that Phil would visit the island for a grilled shad the next night. That began another tradition of suppers and conversation.

* * * * *

In the second week in April, 1963, a spell of warm, clear days, both Frank and Lilly-Belle were home from their colleges for spring break. Frank and his folks got Windermere ready to launch. On Saturday afternoon the Grants pushed the hull on its rollers down the beach into a high tide, stepped the newly varnished mast, adjusted the stays, mounted the rudder and tiller, and sailed over to the Nomanisan Island dock, where Nonnie and Lilly-Belle got aboard, everyone making ribald remarks about picking up loose women on the side of the cove. Off they went, the five of them, friends on a lark, sipping Nonnie's sassafras tea, glad to be together, happy with the boat and the river and the friendship.

"Life is short, art is long," said Sibyl. "Live it up," said Nonnie. "Carpe diem," said Frank, flush with college words and ideas. "April," said Lilly-Belle, "is the cruellest month." Everyone looked at her for a moment, and she flushed a little, then laughed a little, and everyone else laughed, except Hal, who had the helm, and he said, "Ready about." Then, "Hard a-lee." Obedient Windermere turned through the wind, filling on the new tack. Everyone had more tea.

* * * * *

On Sunday morning Frank got up early, got some coffee, sat on the porch looking down the hill over the housetops to the river. Glad to be home, glad to watch the sun sneaking up out of Maryland, red. Glad to see this clear, fresh day with a breeze picking up, stirring bare budding branches of the lilac in the dooryard. Lovely cool sky.

He heard Hal and Sibyl waking up. He called in, "I'm going sailing. Want to go?" "Not me," said his father. "Sure," said his mother. They rode their bikes down to the shore. The wind was coming out of the northwest. Windermere rode at her anchor, halyards slapping her mast. They rigged the sails. Sibyl took the helm. Frank cast off. They sat on the windward deck. Windermere filled and heeled to equilibrium. They smiled at each other. Peace. The hairline delamination in the mast opened just a bit. Sibyl headed Windermere upwind. As they cleared the lee of the cove, the breeze picked up, unrestrained and gusting. One gust drove the prow deep into the chop. The mast bent. The windward shroud quivered.

"Happy eighteenth birthday, Frankly!" Sibyl beamed on her son. "I've told you before, and I'll tell you again, you are a child of love."

And Sibyl told Frank the story she had told him on every birthday since he was ten. "Frankly, I don't want you ever to forget it. In 1944, mid-July, I had just finished my A-Levels and was still living with my family near Lake Windermere. I rode my bike down to the lake. At the dock I saw this pre-portly, handsome man renting a sailboat. I said 'Cheerio, skipper.' When he looked at me our eyes did acrobatics. We talked. I found that he was an American naval officer. He invited me to crew for him. Then we were out on the lake under sparkling skies, just like today, a spanking breeze. That's why we named this boat Windermere."

Frank watched his mother checking the shoreline, gauging distances, deciding to come about and head back downwind toward the cove. In the brisk wind, Windermere was now partly planing, partly bucking, skipping from wave-top to wave-top. The rigging keened. Sibyl held a steady course.

"We talked about the war, the awful war. I told him I thought that some Americans still didn't give a damn for this war. He said, 'Frankly, my dear, I do give a damn.' Then he told me that he was being transferred to the fleet in the Mediterranean. For the next three days we were inseparable. On the third day, near sunset, we were married by a magistrate, right there on that rental sailboat dock. He had to go back to his base the next day. Very short honeymoon. He shipped out two days after that. I picked up where I left off, but all was so different, because nine months later you were born, a few weeks premature but strong and healthy. When Hal left the Navy after the war, he brought you and me, my Frankly, back here. This has been good. Life is good." Frank looked up at the clean white mainsail and jib full against clear blue sky. Windermere pressed on, passing Nomanisan Island.

A heavy gust scudded down, smacked the sails. The shrouds resisted. The mast bent. Rotten, stressed wood separated. The mast buckled. Frank saw his mother shove the tiller hard to leeward to dump the wind. Windermere rounded up into the gust. Frank saw the masthead swinging down. He saw Sibyl look up just before it crushed her skull.

* * * * *

Watching Frank and Sibyl sailing past the island, Nonnie saw Frank scream, scramble aft, rummage under the wreckage, find his mother, and cradle her broken, bloody head. She shoved off in her skiff, soon came alongside. Frank wept. She towed the death-boat ashore, called the rescue squad, called Hal, then Brad and Emily. Couldn't get Phil, out of town. She called the funeral place and got Hal and Frank into a meeting with the funeral director and a pay-to-pray minister. With some coaching from his friends, Hal set the funeral for Wednesday.

Frank said through his tears, angry, "Reverend, why did God let my mother die?" "Frank, God did not just let your mother die, he wanted her in her heavenly home. He takes the best first. You should take comfort from that." Nonchalance gripped the arm of her chair. Her eyes narrowed. Hal stared through the window at a mourning dove on a phone wire. "One of my friends at work says that people die because they have done something bad and God punishes them. Is that true?" The minister nodded. Nonchalance got up so fast she upset the chair. "Frank. Hal. You come with me. Now. You must not listen to this. You cannot believe this."

* * * * *

Later that afternoon Emily and Brad stood on the porch of Hal and Sibyl's house, greeted neighbors coming and going, watched Frank slip away, walking up the hill, over the hill, gone. In time all the neighbors were gone. Hal motioned them to chairs. They sat silently. Hal sobbed. "Why?" Brad and Emily's glances at each other showed their own tortured why-why-why, still echoing, five years almost to the day after Brad's brother did what he did.

After twenty minutes they were still silent, Hal still sobbing. Soon he was not shaking but speaking in a small voice, slowly, punctuated with sobs, "Your brother." "Yes." "Why?" "We don't know." "How long?" "Forever. Still. Right now." Brad and Emily were now standing on either side of Hal, Hal sobbing again. Their hands were then on Hal's shoulders, feeling the trembles. They said, "We're right here, always."

They walked home, fixed some tea, and sat on their back porch. Emily wiped a tear. Brad cleared his throat. Emily said that Sibyl was such a good wife and mother, a good neighbor, and now she gets her skull crushed. Brad said that he had talked to Nonnie, who had gone back down to the Cove to secure the boat and had seen that the mast was rotten where it broke. Even that well-crafted laminate could open a minuscule crack to admit minuscule bacteria to spread into rot. So when the mast took even that reasonable stress, it just broke, and the masthead swung down where her skull happened to be.

Another long silence. Brad said, "After my brother, the only answer I ever heard that even began to answer the 'Why?' came from Nonnie. She said he was born that way because chemicals and genes and hormones combined the way they did. They just did, long before he was born."

Emily: "We were looking for some big existential reason. Nonnie doesn't have a God at all, so she says that natural laws just operate indifferently." She stood. "It leaves us still wondering where God, if any, fits into our lives, if at all." They gazed at each other, a deep sadness exchanged, but strangely mitigated in the gazing. This had happened before. It's why they kept bringing up this most painful of all matters, and talked it out, week after long week.

* * * * *

Hal sat crying. After a while he got chilly, went inside his fine big house, all by himself, and started to get outside a bottle of Virginia Aristocrat, bottled-in-bond straight bourbon whiskey, ninety proof.

* * * * *

The funeral director's minister put on a wretched funeral. Nonchalance sat in the back and closed her eyes. She might have been praying, or communing, or whatever. But she was there. This minister went on at length about how God had called Sibyl home and how she was in a better place. Frank nearly walked out. The funeral home piped in lugubrious sounds, and everyone left feeling worse than they had when it all started.

The neighbors had laid out quantities of food in the Grants' big empty house. Emily, Brad, and Nonnie brought Hal and Frank back for a gathering, so for a while that afternoon things got as good as they were going to get for a long time.

* * * * *

The next week Phil got home and heard about Sibyl's death. He went to visit Hal and Frank. They both looked awful, sleepless, unshaven, dressed in raggedy stuff, barefoot, trying to get the coffee-maker to work, snapping at each other. Phil asked whether they would like to sit and talk. Frank said no he did not want to sit or talk. He started for the door. Hal's flushed face and clenched fists showed fierce rage. "Yes you will. We're going to talk this through." Frank was shaking his head.

"Phil," said Hal, "I've told Frank here that we're going to get some answers from you and he's going to listen. So sit and talk. Frank, sit." All sat. "Frank, listen. Phil, all our lives my Sibyl and I heard all that good stuff about God's love and now she's gone and you've got some explaining to do."

Phil took a deep breath. "Tell me, please, what questions you'd like me to explain." "Why did she die?" "Hal, this will be brutal, because I don't have any sugar to coat it with. Do you really want to do this now?"

"Yes, now. As brutal as you want, because I am angry with you, with God, and with Frank." He sighed, continued. "And if having her cut off from her young life wasn't enough, it happened on

Frank's eighteenth birthday which was also your wonderful Easter Sunday. How gross is that? Some God you have there."

Phil remembered someone saying that grief disconnects all the rationality circuits. He also remembered that, when he grieved once upon a time, a certain Samaritan had talked candor and raw reality. That hard kindness had helped start his own return to sanity. Another deep breath. He began. "Have you heard what Nonnie said about the mast?"

"No. What about it?" "It was rotten inside. She could see where the laminate had cracked and rot had worked through it. The stress broke it at the weak place and the masthead came down on Sibyl." "Oh. God. Oh no." "Oh yes." Frank had closed his eyes. They leaked grief and despair and now a horrible realization.

Phil: "Sibyl died because laminates separated, water carried bacteria in, bacteria ate the wood fiber, rot weakened the laminates, wind stressed the weak spot, the mast broke, gravity pulled the masthead down to where Sibyl was sitting and struck her a lethal blow."

"No," said Hal, his engineering mind not functioning very well, "God took Sibyl because she was truly special and he wanted her home in heaven. The other reverend said so." Phil wanted to say, The other reverend needs to grow up.

He said, "Hal. Look at me. God weeps with you, right now. God did not orchestrate those physical forces to snatch Sibyl out of this powerful marriage and parenthood and friendships. No." "Then why did she die?" "I just told you. The masthead crushed her skull." "Why?" "Because she was sitting in its swinging arc." "Why didn't God make it miss by an inch, just one lousy inch?" "Because God doesn't break the natural laws that keep the universe stable and predictable." "Oh please."

* * * * *

Phil left as best he could and went across to Emily and Brad. "Well," he said, "Hal told me where to go and how fast." Brad made them each a Tom Collins to toast Sibyl. And Hal. And Frank. He said, "Make it last, people, it's like life, you only get one and you'd better get everything out of it." That was good for a wry smile or two, but they sipped carefully and spoke carefully, full of care for this hard moment. Phil admired them. "As far as I'm concerned," he said as the three stood facing one another with their backs to the world, "I've said all I can say about this damnable situation."

* * * * *

In time, Hal got himself back to work, but only to work, coming home to close himself in his paneled den with his Bourbon friend, the faithful Virginia Aristocrat the Fifth, his ninety-proof pain-killer. Frank got himself back to the university and stayed there for summer school with his own friend, Ginny the Beefeater.

* * * * *

A month later, Phil gave Brad and Emily his news. He said, "Friends. An announcement. The Vietnamese war has left many orphans." They nodded, puzzled. He continued. "I have accepted a position as manager of a network of orphanages in Vietnam. I'm flying out next month." "Oh Phil." Emily seemed near tears. He pressed on. "I hate to leave." Their faces and bodies slumped. Phil went on. "You are special, wonderful people. I love you." He went to tell Hal. Then Nonnie. "And please write to keep me up. I'll be back."

* * * * *

Hal's bladder got him off the daybed in the basement rec room where he had slept since Sibyl . . . since Sibyl . . . . He couldn't say "died," he said "left." On the way by he visited his bottle. "Bottle," he said, "Frank did it. Frank never noticed that crack all those years he varnished over it. God. No."

* * * * *

With the addition of these three characters, we have the whole cast. Brad and Emily may appear to be two ends of one ping pong table, but read on. I gave Phil Imbroglio a name like that because I think that any decent parable needs evocative names for people and places.

3   Compounded Alienation

On a Saturday morning in early October, Lilly-Belle came to Nomanisan Island and found Nonnie canning vegetables. "Ma. Ma." Lilly-Belle was in tears. "I'm pregnant." On the bare planked porch of the shack, Lilly-Belle took the glass of water from Nonchalance, drew close to her mother, and began. "Frank got me drunk. I'm pregnant." "That's obvious," said Nonchalance.

Lilly-Belle told her story in bits. Two weeks after the funeral Frank called her from the university. Still so angry and depressed about Mrs. Grant. A dance on Mayday weekend. Could she come down? "No, I have papers and exams coming up." "Please, I'm so lonely and depressed. You can stay with Sam's folks in town. Louis Armstrong. Go back Sunday afternoon."

"I couldn't resist. We have fun. I felt sorry for him. I caught the Saturday morning train. He took me to a party. Ma, he was so angry, I've never seen him like that, even that night after she was killed. Gave me moose juice. Gin and pineapple juice. Never knew what hit me, woke up just before dawn. In his bed. Dressed, walked to the station, took the first northbound."

Mother and daughter watched a gull circle near the river, swoop, flap off carrying detritus. Sunlight sparkled from wavelets stretching south to the marshy peninsula and beyond, down to the houses on the shore a mile or so away. "Ma, when I missed my period, I went to the university clinic and they said yes, you are pregnant and your blood pressure's up, take it easy. I just couldn't tell you, Ma, so I kept on my course work and that's why I never came home all summer. When I told you I was doing research, I

21

was, and I took more summer school. But in August I felt awful and my legs swelled up last week and I couldn't see clearly. I went back to the clinic. My blood pressure was way up and the doc said I have something called preeclampsia and I have to go to bed or I'll have seizures and lose the baby and maybe a stroke and maybe die. What do I do, Ma?" "You go to bed. What does Frank say?" "He's really angry now. Says too bad about the baby. We're not married, and it's not his problem." "It's his problem. You and Frank will be married next week. Believe it." "But my scholarship! My doctorate!" "Can wait. Your body and baby get your full care."

Nonnie took Lilly-Belle into the Fiery Furnace and helped her into the bed where the Nick-Nonnie nexus originated Lilly-Belle in the first place, tucking her in and assuring her. "Stay still, Lilly-Belle. I got this thing."

Nonnie left Nomanisan Island and strode up the hill to Bon Vivant. She strode up Hal's front steps. Knocked. Hal greeted her, but the door opened not wide. "Hal, we gotta talk." Hal stepped out and led Nonnie to a pair of Adirondack chairs. She sat. He sat. Silence. Both stared over the trees stretching down the hill, down to the river, stared at this crisp, clear fall day, sun one quarter up over Maryland reflecting from the wavelets.

Nonnie spoke. "Lilly-Belle just came home. Pregnant. Very ill. Preeclampsia." Paused. Wondered whether Hal would empathize, or what. Waited for his response. He stared at the river. She breathed audibly. He shifted to face her. "Who?" "Frank." "How do you know this?" "Lilly-Belle told me." "Of course she would."

This crack enraged her. Hot flush. Gut turned. Adrenaline rushed. She stood, straightened. "Hal." She looked down at the marsh, her marsh, her demi-paradise, now fallen. It blurred through tearing eyes. She looked at Hal. Deep breath. Centered herself, ordered her thoughts.

Hal's body retracted into the Adirondack. Nonchalance McFinn went down on one knee to come face to face with Prince Hal. "Harold Grant. Your son admitted it to Lilly-Belle." She paused. "Hal, Lilly-Belle could die. She needs home care. They need a home, not that shack on the island. They need you. They're getting married." Nonnie watched Hal react. He shrank farther into the Adirondack. Never a big man, he now appeared to her to dwindle into grief, anger, fear, loneliness. She saw these noxious forces leach his character. She thought: God, he's Lilliputianizing.

"Hal, I'll be here every day to take care of her. Before I go to work. I've got to work." Silence. Brooding. Staring at the river and the marsh and the past, the long-gone past. "Hal?" Silence. A breath of breeze stirred some fallen leaves.

Then Vesuvius, Krakatau. Hal stood, staring at his feet, shoulders sagging. Nonnie stood, saw Hal's face blanch, hands shaking, eyes rolling up to hers. She watched him point two fingers at her face. "Never! Sibyl's dead. Frank killed her. Get out. Sibyl's dead. His fault. Never." Nonnie backed down the steps. "Tell him," Hal shouted, "this is the end! Don't show up here again! He killed my wife! Don't bring a wife to this house!"

* * * * *

At about the same time, in Charlottesville, Frank left class, strolled to the Corner with three friends, had a beer at the local, decided on a road trip to Sweet Briar, had another beer, went to the gym, played some handball, took a swim, strolled to his rooming house, looked for his history text, lay down, fell asleep.

* * * * *

Nonnie walked to the store, bought food for Lilly-Belle, returned to the marsh, fixed lunch for Lilly-Belle, walked to the train station, caught the afternoon train to Charlottesville, and snoozed.

From the train station she walked to Frank's rooming house, found Frank asleep, rolled him onto the floor, knelt her two hundred twenty pounds on the small of his back, a shock of his bushy hair in her angry left fist, his right ear in her angry right fist, and twisted till Frank swore a promise to marry Lilly-Belle day after tomorrow out on the end of the dock that the two of them had repaired when Lilly-Belle was fifteen and Frank was twelve. "You remember how you two towed driftwood boards off the river? You remember how you knocked nails out and straightened them and used them again? You remember how I brought you cool water, and your mother and father came down from the hill and admired what you kids did together?" "Yes'm." Nonchalance also remembered for Frank all the years of Frank the rich kid playing with Lilly-Belle the poor kid. Nonchalance got a solemn promise out of Frank to honor that long covenant.

"Now, please, Miss Nonnie, let me up. You're hurting me." "Tough," said Nonchalance, "you've hurt your best friend, and you've hurt me, and now we're going to get some justice into your spoiled brat life. Tell me again exactly what you're going to do, and when." "I'm going to leave the university after exams and . . . ." Nonchalance twisted both fists. "You're going to leave the university immediately after I get off your back." "But my grades. My father." Nonchalance twisted again. "Your baby, your wife, your housing, your income. So what are you going to do starting tomorrow morning?"

"I'm going to build a place to live." Nonchalance relaxed her grip. "And next?" "I'm going to marry Lilly-Belle." "Next?" "I'll get a job." Nonchalance let go of Frank's hair and said, "You miss your mom, don't you." "Yes ma'am." "I do too. She was my friend." "Can I get up now?"

Frank and Nonchalance packed his gear. They caught the six o'clock Southern to Alexandria. The train slipped through the October evening, beyond the rolling Piedmont into the alluvial plain of the Chesapeake tributaries. Pastures and farmlands and small villages. Nonnie and Frank rode in quietude until Nonnie opened the hard topic. "You got to talk to your father." Frank wouldn't respond. He wouldn't talk.

The train pulled into the Alexandria station. They humped the gear down to the river. Nonnie fixed supper by the old kerosene lamp-light. Afterward Frank said he didn't want to go home. Nonchalance said he could sleep on the porch tonight and go to see his father tomorrow. On this chilly October night Frank wrapped himself in his only blanket and lay on the porch planks way down the hill from Bon Vivant.

Frank's thoughts gave him a hard, sleepless time. Dark snatches and fragments bubbled through sub-conscious, semi-conscious, self-conscious. This island, this cove, this river. First illicit sail with Lilly-Belle. Perfect sail with Mother turned nightmare. Half-remembered night in Charlottesville with Lilly-Belle. Rising engineer like Father turns dirt-low laborer. Lilly-Belle pregnant. Rare disorder, maybe lethal. Fatherhood. Husband. Talk to Father. Tarpaper shack. Trip to Sweet Briar. Bull briar. Life in the bull briars. The big boy cried himself to sleep. Hours later the sun came up over Maryland and struck him awake.

For breakfast they all sat on the bed and ate the last of the cold cereal and a half-mug each of boiled coffee, straight. Lilly-Belle lay in the Fiery Furnace. Afterward, Frank started building the shack on the next little hummock, on stilts too. Nonnie borrowed a friend's pickup so Frank could forage in the construction sites for cast-off lumber, old scaffolding, bent nails. Nonnie rowed around in the skiff dragging in driftwood planks.

The evening of that first day, Frank told Nonchalance his hands were too sore to go on, and why couldn't he have finished the semester and what's the rush anyhow. Nonnie took him into The Fiery Furnace with Lilly-Belle.

"Lilly-Belle, you had no business going to Charlottesville, and you know it. Frank, you had no business jerking sympathy out of her even if you were grieving your mom. And you had no business giving her that moose juice." Nonchalance turned to Frank. "You want to know what's the rush? I told you in Charlottesville what's the rush. The rush is that you made this woman pregnant and now she's ill and she could lose the baby or her life or both and you got to house her and the baby and get a job to pay for it all."

She felt herself warming to her subject. "I'm not paying for it. I didn't get her pregnant. You've made her lose her doctorate. She's got to live quietly here and you got to take care of her. I got to work to live, I can't take care of her. Either of you want to quarrel with me?" A hoot owl down the Virginia shore did a "wh-wh-whoooo." It was very quiet on the river. "Now get on with your life," said Nonnie, and pulled Frank to his feet.

By nightfall two days later Frank and Nonchalance had finished the new shack using old lumber pulled from the river and scavenged from construction dumps and nailed together to make a room with a shed roof, covered in tarpaper. Lilly-Belle settled herself on the creaky old castoff bed Nonchalance had found. She hand-printed a sign to tack over it: "Bedlam."

After supper, Nonchalance said, "Frank, it's time for you to talk to your father." "I can't." "You will. I have not yet bequeathed you this homestead on my island, so unless I say you can sleep in it, you can't, and Lilly-Belle will sleep alone. But you can't sleep anywhere else, either, so unless you get yourself up there to your father's house and come back here and tell me what he said, it'll be nothing between you and the cold hard ground but your skin."

Frank got himself across the gut and made his way in the dark to Windermere's beach. Through the mists of memory he couldn't see details, but his memory gave him images of the old boat on its rollers, the bike tire skid marks in the sand, the paint and varnish and brushes, the hot chocolate and brown bread, his bike where he had leapt off, the beholdings of his heart. In these mists of memory, little Frankly got on his bike and rode it backward, up the lane, up the hill, retrogradation and reversion and regression all at once until he backed up the front porch steps and stood, wee child, calling out "Father, Father, it's me, Frankly! Father!"

Hal, in bourbonic near-catatonia, heard the bleating and opened the door. "It was an accident, Father! I don't know how it happened!" Hal looked at his son, tears rising into reddened eyes. "Say something, Father!" Hal wept quietly. Frank said, "I'm gonna get a job on Quander Road. I'll make a lot of money and we'll . . . ." And then Hal did the thing that haunted him for years. He laughed. He laughed aloud, a spiteful laugh with neither humor nor warmth.

When he stopped laughing, he leaned toward his son, pointing at his face, and he said, "And you're going to reverse the rot in that mast and replay all those years you varnished over that crack but never noticed a thing, never noticed. And you're going to bring back my wife." He dropped his face into his hands, sobbing. He slammed the door. Frank slipped back down the steps, back down the hill, back to the island, leaving little Frankly holding both arms up toward the closed father behind the slammed door.

Nonnie heard the account. Frank slept in the old iron bed with Lilly-Belle and their fetus.

* * * * *

Nonnie had a problem. Phil in Vietnam. She trusted no other minister. The wedding must happen. She asked around about whether anyone knew a preacher who didn't preach, who would just hitch two people with no questions. Sure, said her favorite drunk. Try Reverend Sam, down to the Tabernacle. Nonnie found marrying Sam and solved her problem with a ten dollar bill and a little speech: "Say nothing, brother, but the words in the book, nothing else, or else."

The next morning down at the end of the dock, the river out beyond, the sun sneaking up out of Maryland, not red, they all heard the words, " . . . love him, comfort him, honor and keep him in sickness and in health; and forsaking all others, keep thee only unto him, so long as ye both shall live?" Lilly-Belle said yes, Frank said yes. Nonchalance sent the hired minister on his way, grilled a shad on Shadrach, poured the three of them a cup of Ripple, and toasted them saying, "First be, then do."

Frank walked up to Quander Road to the new development, found the foreman, and asked for work. The foreman stood a head shorter than Frank, but still dominant. He pinched out the stub of his Camel between gnarled thumb and forefinger. Frank saw him do it, and winced. "Start Monday. Laborer. Dollar an hour."

Frank had a surge of non-compliance, self-compliance: "Mr. Johansson, that's not enough. I just got married. She's pregnant." "How old are you, boy?" "I'm eighteen, sir." "You're lucky to have a job. When I was your age I got a dime an hour. You'll make two thousand dollars in one year. Work hard, make carpenter's helper, get more money. Don't make trouble or I'll bust you."

* * * * *

Assertive Frank walked back down to the island, where Lilly-Belle had gotten back onto the creaky old bed and Nonchalance was grubbing in her garden.

He walked all over Nomanisan, then rowed the skiff over to the marsh and poked around the shoreline. And there he found, where Nonnie had beached it out of sight, covered with branches blown off in the September windstorm: Windermere. Windermere the death-boat, broken mast and sails collapsed over all, lines and stays jumbled, rudder and tiller twisted loose, two coffee mugs in the bilge water. Frank stared a long time at Windermere. He pushed his way through the underbrush and slogged across the marsh to the parkway. Down to the filling station where he cadged a gas can, a gallon of gas, an old newspaper, and a pack of matches. "I'll pay you in two weeks, Tommy," he said, and Tommy waved him on.

Frank walked back down to Windermere and did what had to be done. He got her afloat, put a dozen skull-size rocks into her bilge, secured her bowline to the skiff's transom, and towed her out into the channel near the Number 90 buoy, a four-second red flasher. He poured the gasoline all over Windermere and set her adrift. He rowed upwind, tied some balled up newspaper to a stone, lit the newspaper, and lofted it like a flaming siege bomb over into Windermere, which went up: cedar-planked hull and deck, oak frames, spruce mast and boom, canvas sails, manila lines, all but the stainless steel stays, bronze fittings, and galvanized centerboard, which sank when the rest burned out.

Nonchalance was waiting for him when he rowed back to Nomanisan Island. She put an arm around his shoulders and walked him to her porch. She handed him an envelope and told him he needed sturdy work clothes for Monday morning. She told him Lilly-Belle should go to the doctor. She told him she would bring them a pot of vegetables and her Dutch oven bread for supper.

She told him to spend time over supper. Frank sat on a log at the water's edge and opened the envelope. Three five-dollar bills. Probably most of what Nonnie got at the farmer's market.

Nonnie got a taxi to take Lilly-Belle and Frank to the doctor. The doctor asked Lilly-Belle about her skin, the blanching and rashes. She said her hands and feet got cold in the shack. He urged her to keep them warm. She heard him talk about something called Raynaud's phenomenon. The doctor examined her for the preeclampsia and told her that it still threatened her and the baby. "Lie still. No stress." She told Frank to pay the doctor with one of the five-dollar bills.

Back at the island, Lilly-Belle got into Bedlam in the new tarpaper shack. It was a still, lovely October afternoon. The river lay calm. Frank hiked up to the Good Will store on Duke Street and found some work trousers, heavy shirt, wool hat, sturdy gloves, warm sox, and boots. There was a good jacket, but his remaining dollars wouldn't pay for everything, so he left it.

That evening turned chilly. "We need a stove," Lilly-Belle told him. Frank looked at her. He stripped and lay down on his side of Bedlam, soon snoring.

* * * * *

On Monday morning Frank got into his new-old work clothes and walked to the construction site through a ground fog under overcast, heavy cloud cover, about thirty-five degrees. At the chuck wagon he bought four sweet buns and a cup of coffee, paying one hour's wage. Mr. Johannson set him to carrying nails and lumber to the carpenters.

Then it started. The other laborers harassing. The carpenters bossing. Mr. Johansson yelling. "Move it, boy! Get them nails up there now! Yes, sweety, the whole keg!" For lunch he bought three foot-long hot dogs and more coffee. He paid half of the wages he had just made. That left him, he figured, two hours of wages for himself, which had to go to buy supper. But he'd make four hours in the afternoon.

Frank reported to work on time every day and proved himself a model of compliance.

* * * * *

On a Sunday morning in November, the rising sun got Hal awake. The first morning back in his old bed. Morning, the worst time of the day, the time of death-memories and sensations and sounds. Hal lay far over on his side of the bed to distance himself from the other side of the bed, his grief-wallow, his daily adversary and nightly demon. He snuggled up to his Sibyl-phantasm. Her wraith, ever-present, smiled that lovely rosy-cheeked smile, and Hal had one of those unbidden glimpses back eleven years to her sibylline remark, "I thought you were going to get these strips in cedar. This looks like spruce." Why, he asked himself yet again, why does that remark haunt me?

In her first letter to Phil in Vietnam, Emily wrote, "Now, as to Hal. After you left, he continued holed up in his house, an emotional hermit. When we invite him to supper or anything else, he declines. We never see him except leaving for work and coming home." As to Frank, she said, "he is a teen besotted with grief-driven anger, testosterone-driven urges, and alcohol-driven irresponsibility. Now he's wrecked his childhood friend's promising schooling, he has derailed his own pretty-good progress, and he has devastated his already broken father-widower. Aside from that, good Phil, things are okay here. Come home soon. We need you."

4 Bootstrapping

On a cold December day Lilly-Belle lay very still on the old bed in her shack on Nomanisan Island reading *Walden*. She thought about life, and death: the life within, the new life, the child of Frank, as unwanted as she unwanted Frank. And the death she faced if her blood pressure climbed higher. First the seizures. She had read up on preeclampsia and she knew that it rarely kills. But still. She had also read up on Raynaud's phenomenon and cursed the cold.

Lilly-Belle felt less sorry for herself than angry at Frank, and angry at the mast that rotted from the inside, and angry at God who let it all happen. Or maybe even caused it all. One of her friends had told her that God never gives us more than we can bear. And that God gives us hardships to build our character. And that it says so right in the Bible, right here on this scripture card. Lilly-Belle thought it was amusing: how childlike her friend was to rely on this ancient folklore as though it spoke to anyone other than the people who wrote it. But she had kept the card for a bookmark, and now she looked it over again:

"We glory in tribulations also: knowing that tribulation worketh patience; And patience, experience; and experience, hope: And hope maketh not ashamed; because the love of God is shed abroad in our hearts by the Holy Ghost which is given unto us. (Romans 5:1-6, *King James Version)*"

"Gobbledygook," she said aloud. And she thought, Paul was a lunatic. He can glory in his tribulations if he wants. I curse mine. Tribulations produce pain. Period. Her doctoral work cut short before she completed even one year. No chance for the Ph.D. Maybe a master's part-time.

And Frank. Frank, who got me out of university work and into this river shack, pregnant and life-threatened. Frank, who got me married to a developer's laborer with an undeveloped mind. Frank, the jerk. Now my self-serving, self-indulgent, self-righteous husband. Lilly-Belle put both hands over her swollen tummy and cried and cried. She had a splitting headache and her hands and feet hurt in this cold shack.

* * * * *

Nonchalance grubbed up the last of the potatoes from her potato patch and leaned on her hoe, watching an old blue heron glide across the marsh, the sun dropping into the west, backlighting the left-over orange and gold and russet leaves, sending shadows creeping across the cove. "Maybe there is a God, and maybe there isn't. But if there is a God, it's in these trees, and in this marsh, and in these little waves and the breeze and the cattails. It's not some imaginary divinity causing all this pain." A gull swooped down to beg for a handout.

* * * * *

January came and went. On Groundhog Day the sun was rising over Maryland as Frank sat on the edge of Bedlam pulling on his boondockers. Lilly-Belle rolled over and told him, again, that the baby was due on Lincoln's birthday, and they still didn't have the money for the doctor and hospital, let alone a crib and blankets and diapers and what did he plan to do about that?

And then, the morning of Lincoln's birthday, the contractions. And the breaking water. And Nonchalance, competent here as in towing a death-boat to shore, delivered the little daughter. "Rebecca," said Lilly-Belle. "She's Rebecca. I like Rebekah at the well. Generous. Hospitable. Like you."

* * * * *

Frank hardly noticed when Rebecca was born, he was so tired, and so preoccupied with being the helpingest helper. But Lilly-Belle never let up: "We need diapers. We need baby food. We need firewood. Get more work."

Frank cut back on the chuck wagon fare and started having Cheerios for breakfast and taking instant coffee in an old thermos that floated up from the river and peanut butter and jelly sandwiches. The savings went for diapers and baby food and resentment. He scoured the beaches for some sense of purpose to this stupid existence and some driftwood for the fire.

One afternoon, trudging home, Frank spotted a man cutting up a fallen tree on his vacant lot. "I'll do that for you, mister!," called out the erstwhile University of Virginia engineering student. Strong and fit, he finished quickly, and the man asked him how much and Frank said, just give me the axe and the buck saw and let me come cut again for cash and the man asked how he'd like to clear an entire site where he planned to build a house on speculation, and that got things going.

For the next several weeks Frank spent his free time clearing the site, burning the brush, and using the man's red 1947 Ford pickup to haul off the logs. When the man was ready to settle up, Frank said he'd settle for the pickup, which after all had over two hundred thousand miles and needed a new head, new brakes, new clutch, and the man laughed and said, "Frank, you're a hustler, and I think I'm getting the short end of this deal but you look like you need a little boost, what with the baby and all, so take the truck and be off with you. Take the tools too, but remember that I know where you live and I'll be after you for a favor one of these fine days, my lad. Now git!"

* * * * *

One spring morning on the Quander Road development Mr. Johansson put Frank on a crew of laborers clearing brush, bull briars, honeysuckle, and matted undergrowth on a hillside. Frank stripped himself down to just his trousers and boondockers and set to, whacking away with his brush hook, hauling great quantities of brush to the burning pile, practically jogging back, setting a fierce pace. "I'll show them how a real man works," thought he.

He noticed a new laborer, a big man in bib overalls, a heavy flannel shirt over what looked like a union suit, a beat-up old fedora on his very large, round head, filthy boots wrapped with friction tape, and a bandana around his bull-neck. Frank became indignant at this man's lassitude: stopping frequently to drink water, to sharpen his blade, to wet his bandana and swab his face, swinging at half Frank's rate. After an hour, however, Frank noticed that he and the newcomer were still side-by-side as they worked up the hillside. Frank stepped up his pace.

By lunchtime sweat had soaked the big laborer's union suit and overalls, the evaporation cooling him, so that he looked oddly fresh. Frank sat on a log and nursed a new blister on each hand, feeling blanched and burned, both. Frank had not yet spoken, nor had the man looked his way, keeping his eyes down on his work.

* * * * *

Emily and Brad ran into Nonnie at the grocery store. "How's Lilly-Belle?," Emily asked. "Lilly-Belle worries me," said Nonnie. "She has been dispirited, but more and more she won't or can't communicate. I worry that she had a little stroke during pregnancy."

* * * * *

The next day Frank started working next to the big man. "What's your name, boy?" Frank did not notice the big man's flinch, but he did see the stiffened back. And he heard the low, rich, soft voice and melody, "We are climbing Jacob's ladder," over and over. Then the voice only, "And we shall be free." Repeated softly over and over, eyes fixed on the brambles, the wild rose, the trumpet vine, the wild grape vines, the bull briars, the poison ivy, the honeysuckle, big gloved hands grasping and removing and the big boondockers moving steadily up the hill, swing, slash, pull, swing, slash, pull.

Something arose in Frank. "My name is Frank." "Pleased to know you, Frank, my name is Silas." Eyes still down. Then up to meet Frank's. "Pleased to know you, boy."

Frank gave Silas a ride home in his fine new old pickup. Silas said he came from Georgia. Brought his wife and three babies with him, lived down in Gum Springs, the oldest black community around. He walked the three miles up to Quander Road every morning, and walked back at night. He asked Frank to come round back and meet his folks. Frank tried not to show his shock when he saw the shack with three children and Silas' wife Edna in it. "Best we could find," said Silas. "My grandmammy's place. She lets us live free."

The next morning Frank watched Silas' long easy swing and follow-through, different from Frank's choppy chopping. Silas saw Frank watching and showed him how to run his right hand up high on the helve and slide it down during the swing, till just before contact both arms were accelerating the blade through its arc. He showed him how to aim at just enough brush to whack so that he could follow through and not wrack his arms when the blade jolted to an abrupt stop.

Silas said, "Dumb work be hard, smart work be easy." He showed Frank how to keep a good edge on his brush hook, how to use the hook to pull through a tangle, how to breathe deep and drink much water, how to keep his feet apart for good balance, how to wear layers that would give him choices through the day. Frank the would-be engineer learned some things about the practical economy of energy.

* * * * *

The next day Silas said, "Do this work right, you good for more'n any eight hours." Frank looked a question. Silas said, "We could clear brush for other folks too."

So Frank told Silas about the site he had cleared and Silas said, "If you'd had me beside you you'd have finished in less than half the time and we'd been working another site right now. And I'd been makin' money for little baby's medicine." Frank looked at the strong face with the strong eyes and said, "Let's go, partner."

As 1964 ground on, Frank's life was early up and late down. On weekdays he worked on Quander Road. After hours and weekends he worked with Silas clearing sites. The construction foremen discovered that Frank and Silas could clear land cheaply and well and fast.

One Monday Silas said, "Frank, word is that Mr. Frederickson has bought himself a piece of ground in Lorton to do a big development. Might need clearing. Might need you and me. Might be willing to get us if we offer now." "Yeah? Who says?" "Folks at church." "How'd they know?" "Remember, Frank, our women serve white folks' tables, hear stuff."

Frank forgot about it. Two weeks later he heard two carpenters laughing about Acme Site Prep getting the contract to clear the Frederickson land in Lorton. One said, "Good contract, bad contractors." Frank said to himself, "Hmm. Silas did mention that."

* * * * *

Brad and Emily stopped by to see Lilly-Belle and little Rebecca. On the way home they mused, "Not a happy lady, seems to me." "Yep. Where was the old talk about literature and ideas?" "Nothing but Rebecca, Rebecca, Rebecca." "Not quite depressed, but diminished."

* * * * *

In May, 1966, Frank took the wad of cash he'd squirreled away in a Mason jar buried under a rock behind the shack and was counting it when Lilly-Belle caught him at it. "Where'd you get that?" "Worked for it." "What are you doing with it?" "Going over to Telegraph Road and put a down payment on my new front end loader." "Your what?!" "We're stepping up, Lilly-Belle. You're looking at the new president of Grant Enterprises. I quit my job yesterday. So did Silas."

So little did Frank understand his own wife that he was amazed and speechless when she began to cry, snatching up Rebecca and running to Meshach where Nonchalance was stitching a quilt.

* * * * *

Frank lined up their first mechanized job for early Monday morning. Over the weekend Silas and Frank got the truck going and hauled the loader on the low-boy over to a hillside on South King's Highway where Frederickson Development was putting in a small shopping center. "Strip it," said Frederickson's foreman. Silas stripped it and Frank hauled it. All day and late into the dusk they stripped it. In the morning Frederickson's foreman paid them off and later told Frederickson who said, yes, that's Hal Grant's boy. Pretty good, is he? And Frederickson added Grant Enterprises to his stable of subcontractors.

Frank told Brad this story. Brad told Emily. Emily said, "Let's see. Grant Enterprises got off to a good start, yes. But the way Frank did it, his business gained and his marriage lost." Brad said, "Not such a great balance sheet for the first week."

* * * * *

Hal was sitting in his front-porch Adirondack when Brad and Emily showed up. "C'mon up," he called to them when they were nearly at the top step. They pulled chairs around and sat facing him. "Have a seat."

"Hal," said Emily, "what have you heard from Frank?" This abrupt incursion into Hal's privacy didn't seem to faze him. He looked steadily from Emily to Brad and then out toward the river. "Nothing." "What has he heard from you?" Long pause. "Nothing."

"How long is this going to last?" Longer pause. "Ask him. Want a drink?" "Yes."

Hal was gone a few minutes. Brad and Emily touched hands. Hal appeared and gave each a highball. He said, taking his seat, "Did you hear about the fire in Old Town?" "Yes," said Emily. "And I did ask Frank, and he said, 'ask him yourself, I'm busy. He's not.' So you're the father. How long?"

"Yes, I'm the father, and so it's my business, not yours. Cheers." He raised his glass of amber whisky. Brad: "Our business is being friends and being friends right now is encouraging reconciliation." "Well, Brad, listen up. I am fully reconciled to the demonstrated fact that Frank is a jackass. Drink up." He tipped his glass back, swallowed, coughed, sputtered.

"Hal, it's time to break the chains. You are entitled to all the healthy grief you want, but bitterness is mere bondage. And alcohol has you in chains." "You just can't help preaching, can you, Brad." He started to cry, not much, just little soblets, then moist eyes. "I'm just so damn lonely and nothing makes any difference but this bottled-in-bond Aristocrat." He made a toasting gesture. He turned to them. "Thanks. Everybody else sweeps this under the rug."

Brad and Emily stood. "C'mere, Hal, and bring the rest of that whisky with you." Hal stood and joined them at the railing. Just below them was the lilac bush. Emily got on his right, Brad on his left. Brad said, "Hal, we visited you a week or so after Sibyl died. We noticed this lilac in full bloom. Emily said something about Sibyl dead in the full bloom of her lovely life. You agreed. Now nothing's left of the blooms but full green heart-shaped leaves and . . . ."

Hal interrupted. "When Frank went back to the university after that, I found a little slip of paper in his handwriting. It said, 'When lilacs last in the dooryard bloom'd. An elegy for Lincoln.' He must have been learning something down there." Very long silence. Hal emptied his glass onto the lilac.

* * * * *

"What do you do all the time? You're never home." Lilly-Belle was rocking Rebecca, who was having another midnight coughing fit. Frank pulled off his boots and lay back on the bed. "Make money." "Until midnight?" "Yep. Keeping the loader and truck maintained. Can't do it during working hours." "Rebecca asks who is that man who sleeps here. She meant you." "I'll have to meet Rebecca sometime. Make sure she doesn't mean someone else." Lilly-Belle locked eyes with Frank. A silent minute passed. Rebecca slept. Lilly-Belle carried her over to Nonchalance's shack. Frank slept.

* * * * *

Throughout the beginnings of Grant Enterprises in the mid-1960s, the housing market was booming in Northern Virginia. And Frank rode the boom. After he got the front-end loader, he hired three more men and made Silas foreman over them. He got more men and more equipment as more contracts came in.

Some building firms just called him up to order site work, but others put out for bids. He soon showed great skill in winning these. One evening after a long day he and Silas were subduing a six-pack. "Frank," said Silas, "this new contract. How'd you get it?" "Kept my eyes and ears open. People blab. People do strange things. Strange things tell you stuff. Ask the right people the right questions. Keep my own mouth shut. You do too, don't you, Silas?" Frank looked at his partner, who gave him a straight look back and cracked another beer.

The partners won contracts, met or exceeded the terms, and the cash flowed in. Frank never talked again about how he outbid his competition. When builders gave Grant Enterprises virgin sites to clear, they got back well-graded surfaces of Virginia clay subsoil. And they got them back fast. Frank hired more men, Silas made more money.

Grant's boys wanted six days a week of hard labor for good cash. They got it. Frank never missed a payroll. He also never missed paying Lilly-Belle a minimal allowance for housekeeping and himself a minimal allowance for beer, cigarettes, and lunch. All other income went into a go-go mutual fund. No more mason jars out back.

* * * * *

In the summer of 1967, Brad and Emily paid one of their visits to the young family on Nomanisan. They heard Frank go on about how he was now the president of his own company and only twenty-two. They didn't hear him talk about being the father of a three-year-old. They didn't hear Lilly-Belle say much of anything. They did hear Frank boast that the cash was flowing and he had ample work. But, he said, it was more and more penny-ante stuff, no challenge, no real profit. He yearned for bigger and better things, less being the good guy and more being the successful guy. They listened for quite a while, then headed home. Emily told Brad, "Some yearnings could seep into a hairline fracture in your conscience like bacteria-laden dew." And Brad said, "Maybe that's how moral rot gets started and you never even know it." Emily: "You could varnish over it more or less unawares." Brad: "Whose skull will get crushed?"

5 Making It Big, and Little

Silas brought the first bacteria to the fracture. On a Sunday afternoon in January, 1968, Silas was helping Frank replace a gasket on a bulldozer. He could use the extra twenty dollars. Wife was ill. No insurance.

He said, "Word is they're gonna re-route I-95. Send it down the middle of Mason Neck. And build a whole new town. Biggest thing ever." "Nothing in the papers or on TV about it." "Frank, why would insiders tell outsiders?" Frank said, "Any other word at church, Silas?" "Some." "Like what? What's the rest, partner?" Silas looked skyward. Frank pulled out his wallet, withdrew two hundred dollars. Silas said, "Your stock market gonna crash."

The next morning Frank called his broker. "What's my fund's value?" "Ninety-six thousand, one hundred sixty-six." "Sell. I'll pick up the check on Wednesday." "But Frank, we're bullish." Frank wasn't listening. Frank was making other calls with a faraway look in his eyes. He put Silas in charge of the week's work and by Friday he had a business loan secured by his heavy equipment and a personal loan from a household finance outfit. Together with the ninety-six thousand they totaled a little over a hundred and twenty-seven thousand. Not all of the statements he attested with his signatures on this paperwork were entirely true, but they were not entirely false, either. He also signed a contract to buy a new house on Quander Road. He got an open contingency clause. Settlement in a month.

* * * * *

The Potomac flows south from Misty Cove past Mt. Vernon and soon curves westward, forming a broad peninsula called Mason Neck. A country road runs the length of this peninsula, joining U.S. Route One. This roadway would become the route of the re-directed I-95, which would cross the Potomac on a new bridge, thence up through Maryland to rejoin the present I-95.

Time for rewards, said Frank to himself. He headed for Kendrick Harwood's farm. Prime real estate. Largest property on Mason Neck. Vast waterfront on the south side of the peninsula. Extended up to that main roadway where developers would build an entire planned town. What'll they call it? Manchester?

At the country store, Frank called Kendrick Harwood. "Mr. Harwood, this is Frank Grant. How are you, sir?" "Who?" "Frank Grant. I'm Harold Grant's son." "Yes, Hal Grant. How are you, Frank?" "I'm fine, sir. I'm in the area, and thought I'd come by for a visit." "Come right along. Nobody here but the hounds and me." Frank zipped his new BMW down the Neck Road, then along a gravel road to the old Harwood farmhouse. Mr. Harwood had been born there. Mrs. Harwood came there as a newlywed. Gorgeous waterfront view for a gorgeous woman.

Quite a number of beagle hounds welcomed Frank. Mr. Harwood brought him into his living room. "How's Hal?" "All right, sir. Still misses Mother. So do we all." "So do I miss my Sally." "She had a very long illness, Mr. Harwood. I remember you once told my father that when Miss Sally died you'd want to move up to Alexandria to be near your friends and a good hospital. Well, Lilly-Belle and I have decided to move down here to Mason Neck to get little Rebecca out in the country where she can have her own horse and learn to raise chickens and rabbits. So we thought you might want to trade houses. I have a contract on a house on Quander Road that will be comfortable for you, and I'm ready to pay you the market price for your acreage."

Kendrick Harwood had already tuned out. Lonely, tired, and old, he had been wanting to move from this drafty place with Sally's ghost in every closet. "What market price?" "A hundred twenty thousand for the whole thing, Mr. Harwood." "One twenty? One twenty!" Silence.

"Kenny," said Frank, "did the Washington Post ever print that story about Sally and Stevie Farrier?"

Very long silence while Kendrick Harwood's face blanched. In the fireplace a log broke through and became smoldering coals. "Get a lawyer, Frank." More silence. "Lawyer?" "Lawyer. You need a lawyer to draw up the settlement." Frank stood. "I'll have a cashier's check for a hundred twenty thousand dollars. A week from today." Half way to the door, he said, "Oh, and Kenny, I think you have a power of attorney for Stevie while he's doing his time. He won't mind if I bring along settlement papers for that nice waterfront parcel that he acquired when, you know, he and Sally, um, you know." "Bring the papers, Frank." "I'll do that, Kenny. Mum's the word." He winked and pushed through the beagles to the front door. "And your new house on Quander Road? The contract is for twenty-five thousand, settlement in three weeks." He closed the door gently and BMW'd up the gravel road.

* * * * *

"We're moving to Mason Neck." Frank pulled off his boots and lay back on the bed. No place to sit in the twelve-by-twelve shack. He saw the calendar nailed to the wall. It showed February 12, 1968, circled in red with "Rebecca's 4th b'day." He turned to his daughter. "Happy birthday, Rebecca." Lilly-Belle fixed him with her stare. "Her birthday was yesterday. I haven't changed the calendar yet." "Sorry, Rebecca." Rebecca stared at him.

Lilly-Belle and Rebecca went outside and stood on the step, shivering. Lilly-Belle stared at the icy Potomac, and at Shadrach, Meshach, and, in her mind's eye, Abedwego over the bed in The Fiery Furnace. She stared at the old dock and the footbridge and the frozen mud where spring would return the swamp grasses and cattails and marsh mallows. She yearned for a real house for Rebecca, with insulation and heat. "When do we move?," she said loud enough for Frank to hear. Frank was snoring.

In the morning, Frank told Nonnie she could move with them to Mason Neck. "Move? Thanks, Frank, but this is where I live and this is where I die. I'll move when you carry me out in my coffin."

* * * * *

Frank and Lilly-Belle and little Rebecca moved into Kendrick Harwood's farmhouse a few weeks later. Mr. Harwood moved into the new house on bare ground on Quander Road. Nonnie started using the Bedlam shack for storing her market wares.

* * * * *

In late 1970 Brad and Emily visited the Grants on Mason Neck and heard Frank crow about how he liquidated his go-go fund just in time to buy the Harwood place before the stock market dropped. They heard how construction prices dropped while demand boomed for his prime Harwood land and his site work all over Mason Neck. They heard how he incorporated as Grant International and was building a corporate headquarters near the new interchange serving Manchester. Driving home after this overdose of Frank, Emily laughed, "That guy's stuff is a vast cash cow." Said Brad, "Fiscal teats gushing."

* * * * *

In 1971 Nonnie wrote Phil a news bulletin, reporting, in part, that "Frank has built his dream house on one of those high waterfront points. He placed it where everybody on the river can see his enormous, vulgar monstrosity. He made a separate suite for each of them, with servants assigned to each to provide separate food service, separate entertainment centers, separate transportation service, separate communication service. Rebecca told me that he told Lilly-Belle and her, as they moved in, 'Enjoy yourselves. Let nothing interfere with whatever you want to do whenever you want to do it in whatever quantity you desire. We have arrived.'"

Nonnie went on to tell Phil that Lilly-Belle had lost interest in everything except Rebecca, so she had nothing to say about how the house looked or how Frank equipped it. On the other hand, Nonnie said, Frank had made the opulence of this place his measure of self-worth. And his narcissism. She reported that Frank had named it "Reprise" since, he said, it would return him to his original theme, the sylvan setting of his youth. "Phil," she wrote, "I searched his face and his tone for signs of irony or even self-awareness, but none. The man lives in an interpersonal vacuum, unconscious of others. Maybe even unconscious that other people are people. They are opportunities.

"He and Lilly-Belle and little Rebecca have settled into their three suites and three isolated lifestyles. This lets Frank and Lilly-Belle exist in a sort of self-protective marital detente, an unstated policy of distance to avoid friction, but no hostility. It lets Lilly-Belle and Rebecca get together without Frank's abrasive presence. But now Rebecca is old enough to get uppity. Seems that Frank is now calling her Reb. She seems to like that. So, Phil, that's the not-news. We miss you. Come home. Love, Nonnie."

* * * * *

Frank had a case of nerves. In a few minutes he would preside over the first annual Grant International banquet. He would announce a change that put himself out on a long limb of risk. But from that limb was hanging fruit with rich potential. A brilliant strategy, unprecedented, a bold move to buy his employees' loyalty. He reviewed his notes, stuffed them into a pocket.

He stood at the podium. Delivered four points: One. All full-time employees, including himself, now have equal ownership of the firm. Means that they all take proportional profits. Two. Their prosperity depends on his ability to win top bids. Three. They must commit to hard, competent, loyal work. Four. "Now, you have noticed that every employee in this firm is African-American. That policy stems from my original partnership with Silas Andrew. An announcement: As of tonight he moves from operations officer to vice president. When you hear him say something, hear it as my voice. Silas made Grant International possible. I don't forget that."

He waited through the long applause and cheers. "Now, let me leave you with this: If you want the money we can make together, buy into this deal with your absolute commitment. I will be as loyal to you as you are loyal to me. And don't you ever forget who's boss, and don't forget that little clause in everyone's contract, the one saying that all I have to do to separate you from this deal is send you a little pink slip saying that you don't work here anymore. Then you don't, and you have no recourse, no appealing my decision. Now take it or leave it." The cheering went on, someone said later, for five minutes. Frank had his team.

Silas and Edna joined Frank at a local tavern in a private room. The men liberated a six-pack. Edna drank soda-pop. "Got to work in the morning," she said. Frank said, "When was it you stopped working for the Farriers, Edna? When you started with the affordable housing department?" "Six years ago." "And," said Silas, "she got promoted yesterday to head of the department." They toasted this, toasted Silas, then Grant International and the Manchester project.

* * * * *

A year or so later, Brad and Emily tried to arrange another visit to the Grants. They were able to get together with Lilly-Belle, but Rebecca was tied up in her entertainment suite and Frank was driving a boat down to Len's Crab Shack in Colonial Beach. The visit was short and they drove back to Bon Vivant. Before going home they stopped by to see Nonnie. She said, "Wonderful, isn't it. Nothing but fourteen-hour days making money and wielding power and demanding respect. He gets respect, of a sort, because he pays premier wages, works his people to a frazzle, and fires them if they flag or goof." "But many thrive," said Emily. "He gets people who like high compensation, liberal overtime, and challenge of survival. They may not have affection for their boss, but they're loyal."

Brad said, "Well, in a sort of way. Consider what a colleague told me yesterday. He said he used to work for Frank in Manchester. He said, and this is just about verbatim: 'Frank's employees respect him like a loaded weapon on a hair trigger. You hear people say keep your eyes on your rear-view mirror around Frank Grant, watch what you say, and when. No one asks Frank to stop by the bar for a beer after work. But he can bid. He knows everything about everybody in the competition and he gets contracts. Don't know how.'"

* * * * *

In 1976, on Reb's twelfth birthday, the delivery truck from Motorbikes Unlimited arrived just after Frank got home from the office. Frank fetched Reb from the entertainment arcade in her private suite. "Just step up here, Honey, I've got something for you." Reb wasn't speaking to her dad that week. She slouched through the doorway, pushing past his bulk. She gazed at his paunch and went upstairs.

The delivery man, looking for a tip, had the bike ready on the tarmac, complete with helmet. Reb kicked the tires, looked up at the delivery man. "I wanted chartreuse." The delivery man looked at Mr. Grant, President of Grant International, corporate deal maker, deal breaker. "Go get chartreuse."

* * * * *

On Friday, July 2, 1976, Nonchalance showed up at Reprise and insisted on getting face to face with both Frank and Lilly-Belle. She said, "I want a houseboat." "A houseboat?" "Houseboat. You live way down here on Mason Neck, and I want to come visit you on my own houseboat. You're buying everything else, buy me a houseboat."

Lilly-Belle said, "Ma, we'll buy you a whole house. No need

for a boat under it. You're seventy-six years old. Who's going to skipper this thing?" "I can skipper it just fine."

"Great idea, Miss Nonnie." Frank smiled at his mother-in-law. "We'll go pick out one tomorrow." "Already picked it out." "Just send me the bill." She told Frank she also needed a Grant International credit card to cover the expenses of her craft, and such like. Frank said, "No problem, Admiral."

So the next day Admiral Nonchalance McFinn took the helm of her houseboat, a 1976 River Queen, forty-three feet long, steel hull, three-foot draft, twelve-foot beam, Chrysler 318 inboard, 6.5 kilowatt Onan generator to top up her batteries. "I need to anchor offshore. Don't like shore power." She painted its name on the transom: "My Coffin."

The next morning, Sunday the fourth of July, 1976, the two-hundredth anniversary of American independence, Nonnie motored down to Reprise where, she swore, she would secure her granddaughter's intellectual and emotional independence from the tyranny of Frank's consumerism. She moored at his new dock, climbed to his mansion, found Reb in her private suite, and told her they were going cruising on the river.

Once underway, grandmother Nonnie set a heading down the center of the long reach from Occoquan past Quantico to Aquia, kicked back in her padded captain's chair, and poured some sassafras tea for herself and Reb. She began regaling her twelve-year-old charge about her own growing up. She told Reb that she remembered being a small child named Clementine. Becoming, not sure how, an orphan living on the streets of Washington. Becoming, not sure how, the adopted child of a kind couple, he a doctor, she a philanthropist. Discovering that while life in this upscale family had its advantages, her adoptive mother lacked even elementary motherliness. Realizing that she couldn't and wouldn't stand for this adoptive state. Running away to lose herself back on the streets. Giving herself the name Nonchalance to express her easy relationship with the world. And the last name McFinn because, not knowing her real birth origins, she wanted to be descended from Huckleberry Finn on her father's side and Hester Prynne's

Pearl on her mother's. Nonnie looked into her granddaughter's widened eyes and slack jaw and saw a connection.

* * * * *

Frank's cooperative was working. But stressing him. He had long ago learned to cope by way of a little eye-opening vodka first thing in the morning ("Just mouthwash," he said to the mirror), a bracer at mid-morning, a companionable martini or two over the daily power lunch, "high tea" (he thought that was pretty witty) in late afternoon, and then the social drinking.

* * * * *

Every once in a while Nonnie took Reb on another declaration of independence voyage on My Coffin, adding details to the Nonchalance McFinn narrative. One spring day the sun broke through a low cloud cover as Nonnie steered the narrow channel from Sandy Point past Squirrel Island, heading up the Occoquan to their lunch café. Reb said "Oh, I get it. If I don't like my identity now, just change it to one I do like and live out that new identity. Right?" "Right. But living out the new identity will give your life a new narrative. Make sure you understand the meaning of the new narrative. Shape the narrative to your own values." Nonnie spun the wheel to starboard to miss a large piece of driftwood dead ahead. "Direct your own course. Make choices and choose. Decide. Set a goal and steer your vessel for it. Choose to do, choose to loaf. Every move you choose or don't choose causes more of you to become. You are always becoming. Travel the narrative. Never forget that narrative carries meaning, and discovering meaning improves life, improves wisdom. Travel with the meaning. Make it speak to you. You'll always grow, maybe even grow up."

Reb broke away from this and walked to the taffrail of My Coffin, searching the wake and the river and the shoreline and the seagulls. She walked to the bow, where she leaned over to watch the prow cutting through the Potomac. After a spell she returned to her grandmother at the helm. Nonnie: "Next question: Why do you suppose I chose to take identity from Huck and Hester's Pearl?" Reb looked at her grandmother. "Well?" "Well, go figure out an answer. See you when you do."

* * * * *

On a Saturday evening in late 1977 Frank perched on a barstool in his country club, bathed in well-being and personal priority. Associates surrounded him. He considered moving to the dining room, but ordered a fourth vodka martini and sent it down in three gulps to join a half-dozen bacon rollups and two baked cheese appetizers. He mopped his brow and loosened his tie. He moved his arms to relieve a vague ache in his shoulder. He pulled in a deep breath but got little. He wondered why his jaw hurt.

Lilly-Belle got the phone call not much later and told the doctor that she was sorry she couldn't drive to the hospital right now but yes a triple bypass sounded fine and would he please call back in the morning.

* * * * *

Frank became conscious of becoming conscious and from the nurse heard about the triple bypass last night. Later a cardiologist explained that Frank's coronary-vascular system had rebelled against its high-stress, high-cholesterol, high-blood pressure, high-alcohol environment and had just seized up.

In a few days Lilly-Belle, Reb, and Nonnie came in with the cardiologist, who announced that Frank would be discharged in the morning. He lay down Frank's new law of life. Off the juice. Physical therapy. Forty-hour work-week. Lighten up. You survived this but you won't survive the next. You choose. The doc left. The family left. The next day Frank went home in a taxi.

* * * * *

Frank did check in at the local Alcoholics Anonymous and within a year had a grip on his drinking. He said to himself that Grant International had brought him wealth, pleasure, and power, but no joy, no peace, no real respect. These he yearned to have, not to replace the wealth, pleasure, and power, but to add to those addictives, his only addictives now that he had given up the hooch.

And so Frank decided to go to church. On a Sunday morning in late 1978 he headed his most recent BMW for the Manchester Bible Church. The music was moving and rousing; the prayers were earnest and personal; the preacher was, well, thought Frank, that preacher said things I really needed to hear. Back at Reprise, he ordered his brunch served on the upper balcony. "Eggs Benedict. Bring champagne for Mrs. Grant, Perrier for me." He dialed Lilly-Belle's suite on the intercom to invite her to join him. "What's the occasion?" "I dunno. Just come on, will you?"

After they had settled into their recliner chairs overlooking the river, Frank gave Lilly-Belle a level look and said, "Lilly-Belle, I've found it. Found what's been missing. I've been unhappy, dissatisfied. Now I see why. The preacher this morning explained it all and . . . ." "The preacher! What have you been up to, you sly fox?" "I went to church this morning. The preacher said to us, and I remember his words, 'The world may reward you for what you do no matter how many commandments you break. You may have collected all the toys because you are good at what you do.'" Frank leaned toward Lilly-Belle. "'But God will reward you with happiness and peace and joy according to how many of his commandments you obey.'" Frank got a dreamy look. "That's the secret, Lilly-Belle. I haven't obeyed all the commandments. How many are there, Lilly-Belle? It's ten, right? Or twelve. There's twelve something." "Ten commandments, Frank. You saw the movie."

"The movie. That's it." He pressed the call button. "Yes, Mr. Grant?" "Video, please. A movie called 'The Ten Commandments.'" "Ten Commandments, sir, coming right up." While they waited, Frank said, "Sure it's not seven? I saw a movie about seven something. Ten seems a lot." "It was seven veils, Frank. Salome's." So Cecil B.

deMille and Charlton Heston introduced Frank to God's covenant with Israel at Sinai while Lilly-Belle returned to her suite and her reading by her pool, the indoor one. Frank pondered these commandments and saw how easily they simplified right and wrong.

The next day he stopped in Manchester to find a book titled *The Bible and How to Obey Its Laws*. Walking toward the bookstore, he spotted a young man, unshaven, long stringy hair, wearing a t-shirt which declared, "If it feels good, do it." A young woman held his hand. She had flowers in her hair. Frank felt a rush of anger. He stepped into their path, arms crossed, feet spread wide. He glowered at them as they hesitated, looking at the bulk before them. "You people disgrace the culture that has given you the freedom to be who you want to be." It was a long string of abstractions for a mind that had engaged only in material matters for a lifetime. It exhausted his repertoire.

But he felt a rush of righteousness and moral certitude, especially regarding the behavior of others. He continued, "Get home to your parents. Honor them. Cut off all that hair. Take a bath. Dress normally." He strode into the bookstore.

The New Frank had never known such joy, peace, and respect. The joy came from knowing that he was on God's side in the eternal war between good and evil. The peace came from his serene conviction that he was right and holy. The respect . . . well, he was confident that everyone respected his purity.

Over the next months Frank took special gratification from being the good father who guided his daughter away from her reluctance to join his renaissance. "Yes you will go to church with me today, young lady. No argument. Thou shalt keep holy the Sabbath day." Reb had heard this many times since her father's conversion to sanctimony. The first time she heard it she balked, but this wasn't effectual, for he simply cut off the electrical power in her suite. Since then she had complied, doing all she could to make the church-going unpleasant.

On a certain Sunday, however, her adolescent hormones activated her adolescent emotions to produce adamant defiance.

"No." "You know the consequences." "Yes. Do you know the consequences for going fishing all day last Sunday? How did that 'keep holy the Sabbath day'? Holy mackerel?" Frank looked fierce. "God's infinite grace forgives me," said the new Frank. "Oh," said Reb as she closed the door in his face. "Prodigal Dad."

Frank shut off the power to her suite, canceled her credit card, disconnected her phone, and locked up her motorbike. "You're grounded till you go to church."

6 Things Come Apart

In late 1981 Nonnie wrote Phil: "About Lilly-Belle. In those first years she endured near poverty, rearing Reb without a functioning father. She took such good care of the child that she lost interest in everything else. Her literary passion evaporated. She became listless, dispirited, made no friends. I wonder whether she had a little stroke during her preeclampsia. Now she's always in her private suite in that vulgar place, reading light fiction and watching TV. She has every comfort. But she has declined yet further. Her passivity has become deep lassitude. Detente with Frank, indifference toward Reb. Each month this gets worse. Now a complete recluse. She's in a sort of lotus-land dreaminess."

Nonnie went on to say that she had watched Reb in a school play and had a chance to talk with some of her teachers. They told her that Reb learned much and well, reading everything in sight and generating heated classroom discussions. The faculty encouraged these and was willing to overlook some borderline rebellions in return for her lively mind at work among them. She gathered other inquiring young minds around her. She had become a school asset.

Nonnie also reported that as Reb's achievements blossomed, so did her contempt for her father, his hypocritical religiosity and legalisms, his domineering ways, his lofty judgment of his family, his neglect of his wife, her mother. All these and more distanced her from him. Headstrong by disposition, she became yet more so. The more he tried to control her, the less she obeyed. Since he thrived on conflict, just as she did, they amplified each other's destructive features.

* * * * *

In the autumn of Reb's senior year, she boarded My Coffin and blurted out, "Huck lit out for the territory and Pearl endured the stigma of being an outcast child." "Bingo," said Nonnie, "so what?" "So you wanted the freedom to escape the hypocrisy of 'sivilization' and the strength to endure outsideness." Nonnie: "Till now, Reb, you just knew about me, now you know me. Not all of me, but some."

They talked at length about Hester and Pearl. They concluded that maybe these two endured because Hester served others and Pearl grew up in her mother's steadfast love, growing a pearl of beauty around the irritant stigma of bastardy. And they talked about Huck and how he grew up as he saw inside the hypocritical culture along his river. And how maybe cruising this river could help Reb grow up.

The houseboat chugged along up the Occoquan. They docked at their little café for lunch, crabcake sandwiches. Nonnie lifted her glass: "I shall drink life to the lees," she said. "And the windwards," added Reb, both laughing.

* * * * *

In January, 1982, as Reb approached graduation, her counselor, frustrated that Reb had applied to no colleges, told her that the faculty would give her a strong recommendation to anywhere in the Ivy League. Reb just sniffed. "I have other plans," she said.

In early May, Reb said to her mother, "I have something to tell you." And she laid out these other plans. When she finished she watched a single tear emerge from each of her mother's big sad eyes and roll down her high cheekbones. Reb noticed, again, the strangely stretched hard appearance of her mother's swarthy skin. She took her mother's hand. They sat, still and quiet. With her hard-skinned hands, Lilly-Belle touched her daughter's ruddy Anglo-Saxon cheeks.

* * * * *

Like other intense intellects, Reb needed down time to re-focus. The school's tight schedule both nourished and exhausted her. So throughout her four years of high school she took time off whenever she wanted, presenting to the dean of students a note on her father's stationery excusing her for various purposes that the dean would deem reasonable. She forged these as needed. One could not tell her forgery from her father's known handwriting, so skilled she had become. Whenever she had to wait for her father in his outer office, she distracted his secretary enough to liberate some current letterhead.

This system served her right up to the day before graduation. In early afternoon the dean called Frank to tell him that Reb would receive a citizenship award for her contributions to the intellectual life of the school. The dean wanted to tell Reb himself, he said, but Frank's note to the school that morning had excused Reb for the afternoon to work in her father's office. "It did?," said Frank.

Too late for the school to rescind the award. Too late also for Frank to repossess the new Kharmann-Ghia convertible, custom painted chartreuse, which he intended to give Reb as a graduation present the next day, because on her afternoon off Reb had taken a little reconnaissance trip on her chartreuse motorbike, found the car in Frank's garage at Reprise, the keys in his top bureau drawer in an envelope also containing a note from Frank congratulating her on her graduation and entrance into the world of adults and enclosing eighteen one-thousand dollar bills, one for each year of bringing him, the note continued, such joy.

She left the chartreuse motorbike on the tarmac where she had first received it and drove the chartreuse Kharmann-Ghia to Burke and Herbert Bank and Trust in Alexandria to deposit the eighteen thousand into a new account, then moved into her new digs on My Coffin, hoping that right about then Frank would be opening what she had nailed to the door of her now-vacant private suite: a manila envelope containing her cut-in-half credit card and a sheet of ninety-five reasons that she could no longer live under the same roof with him. And she even had time to take the Kharmann-Ghia to an automobile repainting place to have it changed to royal blue. The next day she didn't show up for graduation, or the citizenship award.

*****

You may have noticed that Lilly-Belle had symptoms of a skin disorder early on. I have let these lead to a terrible medical situation. She makes her own decisions about her condition and intentions. That's fine. But the physician and Frank do things that should never happen. More on this later.

*****

Within a month of Reb's graduation, Lilly-Belle was feeling awful. Her fingers and toes were swollen, making her skin hard, tight, and discolored. They ached and felt numb. She had trouble breathing and swallowing. She sometimes thought she was strangling on something molten. She took a taxi to the doctor. The doctor said that her Raynaud's syndrome had led to systemic scleroderma, not curable and often fatal. "Fatal and incurable?" asked Lilly-Belle. "Often," said the doctor. "Pain?," asked Lilly-Belle. "Frequently severe," said the doctor. Lilly-Belle interrogated the doctor in reasoned tones. She called a taxi and made her way to Nomanisan Island.

Nonnie put her to bed in Meshach. Lilly-Belle said to Nonnie and Reb, "This is my home. I was born in this bed, I will die in this bed." Reb said, "And Dad?" "Tell him whatever you want. If he even notices I'm not at Reprise. He is not welcome here." They talked long. They hugged, three women facing the future. Lilly-Belle said, "Now hear this. When I said that I would die in this bed,

I mean that and no more or less. No hospital, no efforts to sustain my life. I want to die, and I want to die soon. And here."

The next day Frank did notice that Lilly-Belle was not at Reprise. Panicked, he drove to Nomanisan Island. Nonnie and Reb were not there. He found Lilly-Belle unconscious on the floor in Meshach. He called the emergency squad. At Manchester Hospital, the resident admitted her.

Reb and Nonnie showed up in Lilly-Belle's room. They saw Frank sitting with two older men, one in a dark suit, white-haired; the other in a white lab coat, bald. Lilly-Belle lay unresponsive. The resident, a young wiry man attending Lilly-Belle at her bedside, greeted Reb and Nonnie. "Please come with me," he said, and took them to a conference room.

Nonnie said, "Who are those men with Frank?" The resident explained that the dark suit had said he was a minister from Mr. Grant's church, and the white lab coat was a doctor with privileges in the hospital. Reb recognized him from the country club.

"But," said the resident, "you should know that Mrs. Grant is in grave condition." He explained that she had developed scleroderma renal crisis, with malignant hypertension. "Incurable. She's dying." "How long does she have?" "Could be drawn out for weeks. Her kidneys are failing, but how fast we can't know." He explained that with aggressive treatment Lilly-Belle could live somewhat longer. "I have told Mr. Grant that we would have to . . ." Frank came into the room. The resident finished, " . . . put her on a respirator, and intubate her. Perhaps start dialysis." Frank said, "And that is what we will do, starting immediately." The lab coat man appeared behind Frank. He said, "So, doctor, Mr. Grant has asked me to take on Mrs. Grant as my patient. I'll put in the orders now."

Reb and Nonnie rose as one. "No!" Reb stepped toward her father. "My mother told us that she wants to die, and soon, and on our island, and with no treatments whatever. Nothing. Let her die."

Frank exploded in rage: "Thou shalt not kill!" Reb exploded in rage: "Thou shalt not torture my mother!" Frank: "This is reprehensible! Failing to save life is killing. Thou shalt not kill!"

Reb: "Killing is taking life. The disease is doing the killing. You're protracting her suffering. That's cruel." Frank said, "Killing is killing! She is my wife, I am her husband, no one will kill my wife. Thou shalt not kill." He took a deep breath to gather himself. "The commandments are the word of God. You must not break them. My minister says so." Reb took her own deep breath. "Commandments? What about the one that says to honor your father and mother? I want to honor my mother by refusing to put her through any more pain." Silence. Reb again: "How about the one that says not to bear false witness? You are contradicting the witness she gave Nonnie and me about letting her die under these very conditions. How about the one that prohibits idolatry, worshiping your false god called the Bible? Yes, you are worshiping a book, not the God it tells us about."

Nonnie said to no one, "Who is this amazing person? Where'd she get all this?" Father and daughter stared at each other. Impasse. The resident left. The minister and Frank left, not to return. The lab-coated doctor left and wrote orders to use all measures necessary to sustain Lilly-Belle's life. The staff intubated and respirated Lilly-Belle. Reb and Nonnie took turns at her bedside. One morning, three weeks later, while Reb was away getting coffee, Lilly-Belle died, alone.

* * * * *

This episode is, remember, taking place a quarter of a century ago. It reflects attitudes and practices for end of life situations that did happen then, leading to this frightful scene. But today, I am glad to say, physicians and hospitals encourage patients to have advance directives on file and provide counseling to patients and family about their rights and options. Of course they cannot protect against pain caused when people legally apply their own religious and ethical convictions as Frank did here.

So I hope this episode illustrates why everyone should have a written advance directive and should reconcile religious and ethical differences before the crisis. If Lilly-Belle had written what she merely told Reb and Nonnie, Frank could not have required senseless life-protracting medical treatment to satisfy only his own needs. And if Lilly-Belle had written also that she wanted in-home hospice care, she could have died much sooner, on her island with her family, peacefully, hydrated, without pain or discomfort. Knowing what we know about Frank, of course, we must admit that no amount of talking could have reconciled common sense with his pig-headedness.

Also, having someone with your health care power of attorney ensures that a trusted adult has heard you say what you have written in the directive and can provide medical authorities with the context for your end-of-life wishes.

Any health care facility can provide blank copies of these two documents and guidance to hospice care. Signed and witnessed, they should be on file with a doctor and accessible at home.

So, if Frank had not been so saturated with bogus religiosity, and if he and Lilly-Belle had talked about her wishes, and if he had had the guts to honor them, you might have read this version:

. . . Frank came into the room. The resident finished, "put her on a respirator, and intubate her. Perhaps start dialysis." "No way," said Frank, "she does not want that. What's the alternative?" And the resident explained that a patient with incurable, terminal illness has legal and ethical rights to die with only as much care as needed to maintain pain-free comfort, even when the level of medication needed to control pain may lead to unconsciousness and hasten death. The resident also recommended at-home hospice care. "So be it," said Frank. Hospice nurses made Lilly-Belle comfortable in her own bed on the island. There she died four days later, peaceful, her family around her. . . .

This rendition, however, would not serve the larger issues in my plot, for Reb would not have become obsessed with rage against her father. So what happened next would not have happened. Onward.

* * * * *

In the afternoon of that day of mixed relief and grief, Reb went to a lawyer. "I want to change my name to Rebecca McFinn and I want to renounce any claim to my father's estate." That evening Reb left her father a message on his answering machine announcing what she had done. When Frank called the number listed on the caller ID, she got only another young woman's voice saying, "I'm sorry, she says she's an adult now and speaks only to other adults."

* * * * *

Nonnie went to Lilly-Belle's funeral at Frank's church and found it as appalling as Sibyl's. Frank sat up front, Reb as far from him as she could. Nonnie loitered near the door so she could bolt for fresh air, or so she told people who wanted her to sit with them, but she was keeping an eye on Reb, ready to go to her side and evacuate her if needed.

* * * * *

Notes from Nonnie's letter to Phil that night summarizing the melancholy narrative of Lilly-Belle's dying and the frightful funeral: Lugubrious music. Lugubrious Bible passages in lugubrious tones. From the minister, assurances of Lilly-Belle's celestial bliss mixed with threats of eternal torment for unbelievers and other sinners. "Phil, I fit both of those categories. Do you suppose I'll do double time for double violations? How long is double eternity? How come otherwise intelligent people sit still for such absurd propositions?"

* * * * *

The next day, Emily and Brad went to Nomanisan Island to see Nonchalance and to tell her how sorry they were about Lilly-Belle's dying and the family's loss. "What family?," asked Nonnie. "Frank disgraced himself and tortured his wife. Reb has such deep alienation that even her savvy arguments about letting Lilly-Belle died peacefully just made it worse. And I couldn't get close to either of them. Not proud of that." Then, in a rare show of vulnerability, she poured out to Brad and Emily her sadness over the pathetic isolation in that overwrought house, the over-indulgence, the toxic relationships. She lamented Lilly-Belle's long road from youthful budding intellect to dulled-out middle-aged recluse to pained victim of the rare and mysterious systemic sclerosis. She traced Frank's long road from obsessive workaholism to grubbing greed to unchallenged power to unbounded riches to compulsive commandment-ism. She traced Reb's rebellion, her brilliant achievements and high potential, her anger against her father.

Nonchalance finished with a little speech about how Frank had wrecked her daughter, yes, but she would never hold any grudge against him. "No man is an island," she said. Brad and Emily walked back up to Bon Vivant holding hands, speechless.

* * * * *

7 Things Disintegrate

Cleaning out her mother's suite, Reb felt deep sadness. Then a stunning discovery: a file of manuscripts. On the cover of the file appeared, in her mother's handwriting, "Wellesley's motto: *Non Ministrari sed Ministrare*. Not to be ministered unto, but to minister."

Reb sat on the floor reading at random. Poetry. Short poems, all on the theme of liberty. Psychological liberty, emotional liberty, spiritual liberty. The irony of liberty found in captivity. The hope of liberty. The loss of liberty. Reb read and felt her own deep yearning for liberty from the tyranny of materialism, consumerism, too-much-ism. Liberty from the tyranny of her father's simultaneous supervision and neglect. "Wait a minute," she said to no one, "I broke free from those when I left home." Musing. Silent. "So why don't I have a sense of this liberty?"

Her eyes drifted back to the poems. She wondered about the dates jotted at the tops of the manuscripts, sometimes as many as fifteen or twenty. When Reb opened the next file box she saw the meaning of her mother's life staked out in stark profile: scores of carbon copies of letters written to women in the Virginia state prison in Goochland, with dates from 1970 until her return to Nomanisan Island, letters of kindness and encouragement, always including a poem.

Reb comprehended: her mother, imprisoned in her own marriage, had helped other women endure their own loss of liberty. And she had died in that prison. Reb felt simultaneous pride, sorrow, and anger. The anger grew hot, became hatred.

* * * * *

For several nights after Lilly-Belle's death, Frank lay on his back recollecting his life with her. He recollected their childhood friendship, the tranquility of Misty Cove. He recollected the nightmare of his mother's death and his enraged grief afterward. He recollected inviting Lilly-Belle to Charlottesville, but no images of their time together. Too drunk. He recollected Nonnie's forcing promises from him. And the wedding. And his father's frightful rebuff. Grinding labor. Silas. Risky enterprises. The Mason Neck land acquisition by extortion. The Harwood farmhouse. Reprise. Incorporation. The cooperative scheme. He recollected the three of them in this family not together but each in splendid isolation. And he recollected the commandments of the church, the commandment not to kill.

He relived Reb's assertion that other commandments applied. He could not remember which, or how, but he began having some misgivings over the logical inconsistencies that Reb had raised. He began to wonder why she seemed more right than his righteousness. His commercial mind began to assign numbers to these memories in a mental balance sheet. The items in the liabilities column kept adding up to more than his assets. He began to see his life accounts heavy in the red, and he didn't like being in the red. Something didn't feel right about Reb, what Reb had become and not become in his life.

* * * * *

In her bunk in the cramped forward cabin of My Coffin, with the boxes of her mother's poems and letters in the overhead bin, Reb lay on her back and had some thoughts of her own, equally scrambled. Her young psyche ached to do something to relieve her anger, rectify her alienation and injustice. Grieving for her mother came hard. She loved her mother, but she did not love the life they had lived in Reprise. These opposed feelings intensified her animus toward her father. She hated his repugnant parenting and his cruel, ideological refusal to relieve her mother's agony. These two grievances grew like the suspended roots of a strangler fig, dominating her consciousness until nothing was left but her angry thirst for revenge.

Revenge: she would cause this monstrous man to suffer for his hideous behavior. She brooded. What would be the most painful loss for him? What does he value most? Control, power, influence. Where does he get those? Grant International. Would losing Grant International cause maximum suffering? Yes. If Grant International continued without him at the helm, would that multiply the pain? Yes. But what would cause him to resign from Grant International, leaving the employees as the sole owners and him with nothing but disgrace and humiliation?

Suppose, thought Reb, that the employees discovered that he had only appeared to have such high business principles, such integrity in bidding, and such loyalty to them. Suppose they saw the reality of his self-righteous ethics, his loud-voiced loyalty to his people, and his seeming generosity in converting to a cooperative. Suppose they saw his shadow side, his hypocritical self-interest. Well, she decided, she could arrange to throw back the veil on the dirty truth about Frank Grant, even if she had to make it up. And what would these long-suffering, well-paid employees do when they found that Frank had duped them all these years? Hound him out of office, make life so miserable he would lose all control. Force his resignation. They had a contract for shared ownership and they would take ownership. Yes. Yes.

A second twist in the scheme: Her father must be able to see right away that she, his own daughter, had done this thing to him, that she had gotten her revenge. Then he would have to choose.

He could either protect her, his only child, by admitting to his employees that, yes, he had done the wrongs revealed. This would ruin his own future. Well, that's a joke, said Reb to herself. That he would never do. Frank Grant would never do anything for someone else at his own expense, let alone this.

Or he could ruin her, his only child, by exposing her, which would not only ruin her prospects for employment but also reveal that he indeed would do such a thing to his own flesh and blood to save his own sorry hide. That's what he would do. No doubt.

Resolved. Sound plan. Accomplishes everything. Now for the operational moves. She lay in bed figuring till the moves settled into place.

The next morning she called Grant International and made an appointment to see her father at four-thirty. Around three, she dressed in nondescript jeans and shirt, drove her royal blue Kharmann-Ghia to a side street several blocks from Grant International, and walked to her father's office. She greeted him with cool courtesy. "I had to run some errands down here. Thought I'd drop off this check for my share of the hospital flowers for Mr. Harwood. He's a good friend." She handed him an envelope. "Thanks, Reb, want coffee?" "Gotta run. See you." She tossed a wave and headed for the door, fading from his sight. He wondered about this unaccustomed pleasantness. Liked it.

That night, once again, Frank lay thinking of his encounter with Reb. He had enjoyed this touch of normalcy, a brief interaction of friendship. He felt a novel yearning for friendship with his estranged daughter.

* * * * *

In the morning, as usual, Frank got to the office before anyone else and settled into coffee and day-plans. He heard the first office workers showing up. He got a call from his secretary. "Mr. Grant, I need to see you immediately, sir, may I come in?" She laid on his desk a stapled document. "Every desk in the building had a copy of this when we opened this morning." She left in a hurry.

Frank took it to his easy chair. Thumbing through, he saw photocopies from his appointment books and telephone logs dating back ten years and more. Reading some, he saw notations in his own handwriting, damning notations. He saw notes to himself with reminders to call contacts in competitors' firms, or architectural firms, or government offices asking questions inappropriate and incriminating, demanding compliance with his terms. He read follow-up notes in his own handwriting showing that he had made one sleazy business deal after another to the advantage of Grant International. He saw notes about how he had gotten sensitive data from people who stood to gain as much as he did from exchange of competitive information. All in his own handwriting.

And he saw records of phone calls to certain names with notes like, "How much is Diamond Site Prep bidding?," with a dollar amount in a different ink. Or, "Who knows how much Apex borrowed?," with a name and phone number after it, in a different ink. Many notations like these appeared in the many copies of pages from his appointment books and logs covering many years of Frank's calls and meetings. He found notes about many of his faithful employees saying things like, "Too much sick leave," or "One more smart crack about how much money I'm taking home and he's gone," or "Her hand in the till?," or "Questionable loyalty," or "Drinking problem." Frank's rage surged. He shouted at his desk, "I didn't call those people. I didn't make arrangements like those, not one. I didn't ask those questions. I didn't write those snotty notes. I've been framed."

His secretary called again. "Mr. Grant, I'm getting lots of angry phone calls. And many staff are here to see you about this document." He went out. He heard angry tones, sarcasm, yelling, obscenity, sobs. He saw anger, fear, hurt, disbelief, threat. They were waving the document. He said, "Shut up." Some did. He said, "I've been framed." General uproar. "Go back to work." He strode into his office and slammed the door.

Frank's fog of confusion occluded the next few minutes while he wandered around his office, looking for anything and nothing, finding nothing. From his desk he retrieved his appointment books and phone logs. In them he found the entries he had been reading, all just as he had seen in the photocopies. He thought: Someone got into my desk. Only two keys, one on my belt, a spare hanging at home. Someone who could forge my handwriting. The fog lifted, exposing one stark realization: "Reb."

He stood by the slammed door, the door between him and his

power, his achievement, his people. He spoke to it. "Late yesterday Reb visited me in this office on some flimsy pretext. She let people see her coming in, visiting, and leaving the office. She left this office all right, but not the building. She hid in the building. Did her deed in the dark. And I never questioned the implausible story of errands in Manchester. Or her paying her share of an expense. Or her uncharacteristic concern for a family friend. She used the spare key from home to get into my desk. Took the appointment books and logs. Forged those notes in my handwriting. Copied them and delivered them to other offices all over the building."

A moment of silence. "Just the way she forged all those must-leave-school notes," he said to no one. "Now every employee thinks I've been a sleazy operator." Frank turned to the window to see the sun coming up between two high-rise buildings, leaving the river below it, the river of his joy and his grief. "Unacceptable outcome," he said to the sun, "but easy to avoid." Frank calmed down as he outlined his next steps. "Hire a forensics lab to prove the ink has been out of the pen for hours, not years. Hire a handwriting expert to prove that the notations are in Reb's handwriting, no matter how well forged. Get an affidavit from my secretary that she saw Reb in the office yesterday afternoon. Write up a report of the whole thing. Get my lawyer to validate it. Put it out to the staff to incriminate Reb. Voila, I'm off the hook. My staff realizes that I'm the innocent victim of a hoax. I keep my reputation. Grant International continues untarnished. Justice is done." He walked to the window, the one facing east. "Easy," he said. "I'll call a meeting and tell everyone what happened and how I'll prove it." A warm sensation of self-congratulation washed through Frank's mind as he contemplated how, once again, he had cracked a tough complexity through clear thinking. "Easy. A nuisance, but easy."

He glanced again at the sun between the high rises, those two symbols, for him, of a truism: two sides to every question. He squinted to see the river under the bright sun. "Why?" He squinted yet more. "Why did Reb do this thing? And why, why so easy to figure out? Like she wants me to know she did it to me. Why?" Warm self-congratulation became vague, chilly unease, then troubling doubt. Frank Grant had not made millions through thinking that ignored relevant factors. He sensed a trap just ahead on the path he was planning, this too-easy path that Reb's actions invited him to take. Reb's motives had a relevance here, but what? Frank realized that he must get inside her head to find the trap. "Well," he said aloud, "I'll just call my daughter and ask her." He laughed, an ironic laugh. "Well, not." More pondering. "But," said he, "I can call someone who will talk and who might know."

He called Nonnie. He briefed her on what had happened. He told her that he had concluded that Reb had schemed to wreck his reputation, destroy his livelihood, and force him out of Grant International. "Why, Nonnie, why would she do this?" "Revenge." Frank gasped. "Frank, take a deep breath and hear me out. You and Lilly-Belle damaged that child. Lilly-Belle smothered her with over-protective love and you alternately neglected her, gave her far more than she needed or wanted, disrespected her, and bossed her. The apex of these insults came when you protracted Lilly-Belle's dying. Between the two of you, you pretty much guaranteed she would not mature. Now she's like a small child having a tantrum. She thinks she can rectify her grievances against you by destroying you."

Frank was sputtering. Nonnie said, "Now don't have another cardiac. You called me for something. Was it breast-feeding, or Pablum? Or truth?" Frank had to laugh. "Thanks, you old marsh rat." "No charge. Next: why do you suppose our bright young Reb made it so easy for you to figure out that she has done this thing?" "She did?" "Well, how long did it take you to see through this amateur night?" "Not long." "You think this is the best Reb could do?" "Dunno. She's upset, angry, hasty." "No doubt. But what if she made this deliberately transparent?" "Say what?" "Think, Frank. What's in it for Reb if you know she did this thing to you?"

"I don't know, Nonnie." "Well, make it your business to know. You've told the world for years that you know everything else. Go figure it out. Shed your self-interest long enough to look through someone else's eyes. And call me when you have an answer in terms other than 'what's in it for Frank.'" The line went dead.

Frank stared at the phone for a while, then said to it, "Suppose Reb said, 'Dad, look what I just did to you. What are you going to do about it?' Why would she ask me that question?" Frank had done this sort of thinking in calculating business negotiations, but never in processing the dynamics of family interactions. It came hard. He tried several iterations till he landed on this first-ever insight: "She wanted to be transparent. Wanted me to see that she could do me. Why? First, to one-up her dad. Second, to find out what I would do. Shaft her back? Or shaft myself?"

He lay on his back and thought. "Shaft myself. That's weird. That's Machiavellian." He got to his feet and walked to the window. He pondered. He called Nonnie back. "She set me up to take the blame myself, to give up my own future to safeguard hers." "You got it, Frank. Well said. That's Reb. Now we know just who she is. Question is, Who are you, Frank?" Silence. "Frank, I won't press you for an answer now. That's too private. Consider several answers. Then choose.

"But before you go do something else stupid in your stupid life, take one bit of strong advice from this old marsh rat. Call your father. Don't ask me why I think that's a good idea and long overdue, just do it." Silence. Long silence. "Frank, are you there?" "I'm here. Why should I call my father? He shut me out." "Frank, are you in trouble?" "Yes." "Call your father."

Frank, stunned, hung up, sat for a long, long time. All his memories from the last several nights coalesced around an insight, a flash of realization. "My life is empty. No wife, no mother, no father, no daughter, no friends. Pointless." More pondering, then, "I want to mean something."

Yet more. "Call my father?" Frank contemplated the act. Preposterous. His father had laughed at him and slammed the door. They had not spoken for the many years since. Frank also contemplated Nonnie's deep wisdom over the years. He studied his yellow pad, his options, Nonnie's words. Summed all that, drew it up into a final realization, and made a decision. "All right, then, I'll call my father."

These words brought a rush of fear, a rush of embarrassment, a sick feeling of defeat. Frank sat back down and stared at his feet. "He'll laugh again. Shut me out again. I cannot go dependent again. My father can call me. He knows where I am."

He rolled over into a fetal position and held his head, feeling crushed. He pushed his father from his mind and reviewed his other options. "I can expose Reb, or admit guilt. I can nail her. I've got decisive evidence." Silence. "That's the sensible thing." He pointed to his head. "I can make it public and let her take whatever blame comes her way. And keep Grant International. I could." Silence.

"Or I can take the blame myself. Why would I do that? Reb is young, intelligent, emerging from a hard adolescence which I've prolonged." Silence. "I've had my time. She hasn't. If I finger her, she won't have much future. She'll have a long hard scramble up from disgrace." Silence. He pointed to his heart. "It's the dumb thing to do. It's what I have to do. I'll have to resign. I'll have to shield my daughter."

Frank felt an ineffable sensation of hard loss mixed with rightness. He lay there on the carpet of his office at the base of his plate glass window, peering out at the sky, the sun now over the twin high rises, the river behind.

8 New Realities Emerge

Meanwhile, Reb McFinn had gotten up early to anticipate the grand explosion of justice when her photocopies did their work. She savored the prospect of the demands for Frank's resignation, his humiliation, his retreat in disgrace.

In mid-morning, she called a friend who clerked in the office. Before she could issue her sham invitation to have supper together and catch a movie, she heard her friend's shocked voice: "Reb! Did you hear the news?" "News?," asked the daughter of the doomed president, in fine innocence. "Reb, your dad has been betraying the company and lots of employees for years. Someone collected photocopies of his own appointment books that say so in his own handwriting. Everybody's disgusted."

Reb did an Oscar-grade performance of dismay and tears while she listened to her friend's version of the employees' angry reactions. Reb became more and more gratified at the vitriol reported and the demands for resignation. At length the friend wound down, sensitive to Reb's voice signifying her complete breakdown and incapacity to hear any more and deep need to go and have a good cry before she could get home to condole with her stricken father. Reb's friend promised to call Reb as soon as any more news came out. They hung up. "Perfect," said Reb. "Perfect in every small detail."

* * * * *

In late morning, the president of Grant International stood up, buzzed his secretary to call for an immediate all-hands meeting, packed a briefcase, caffeinated himself, and moved to the big room. He stood before his people and said, "It's all true. I got greedy, I panicked. I snooped for secrets. I manipulated facts. I kept notes on employees. I infiltrated competitors in devious ways. I changed figures behind the scenes." He looked at the shocked faces. "Now I'm resigning effective immediately." Turmoil, tears. Voices: "No." "Yes." "Don't do it." "Good riddance." "Don't slam the door on the way out." Some ambiguous applause.

He walked out. He drove his BMW back to Reprise. He ordered up a tenderloin. He slept. He got his Chris Craft and motored to Cobb Island, where he docked and had a crab feast, all by himself. After sunset he motored back, steering by the Potomac navigation lights, muttering "red right returning, red right returning" and then "Reb right returning."

* * * * *

Around noon, Reb's friend had called, breathless. "Reb. He resigned. He got us together and told us that he had done everything the photocopies said. People were so disgusted they were shouting at him. He said something like don't bother getting mad, I'm gone. I'm out. You can have this company and make something better out of it if you think you can. You'll get along just fine. Goodbye. He had his briefcase with him and he left the building. We watched him get into that BMW and disappear."

By this time Reb was doing more Oscar-work into the phone, weeping and sobbing and saying Oh that poor dear man he must be heartbroken. "No," said her friend, "that was the weird part, he seemed almost cheerful." Reb did not let that shock disturb her Oscar-level role. With a sob, she said, "I gotta go, I can't take it any more, thanks for calling, goodbye." And doing a highland jig, pumping her fists in triumph. "He's gone. He's lost it all. Good."

This euphoria lasted a while, then gave way to nagging misgiving. A wisp of troubling thought, formless. A shape emerging. "Hold on," said Reb, getting electric shudders from head to toe, prickles.

"What about that cheerful bit? He's just lost his life's meaning and he's cheerful?" She deliberated. "I set it up so he would catch on right away that I forged all that stuff. I knew that gave him two miserable choices: He could expose me. That would let everyone see a bum ruining his own daughter to save himself." She sat down on the floor.

"Or he could admit that yes he did do all those despicable things I forged. His employees would lose all trust in his leadership and he would have to resign. When I imagined that option I laughed. No way egocentric Dad would do that." She stood back up. "But now. Now egocentric Dad has done that. Why? All my life egocentric Dad has done nothing but serve his self-interest. Resigning in disgrace does not, not, serve his self-interest. What's going on here?"

Reb's bright young mind began to figure out what was going on here. She struggled with thoughts, writing them down, scratching them out, consolidating, choosing. After a spell, she walked to the window. Over the rooftop across, she saw dark rain clouds and the sun's silver rays penetrating breaks in the overcast. "Whoa!" She sat back down. A possibility emerged. Reb recollected the sacrifices of Abraham and Isaac, of Billy Budd, of Aztecs.

But self-sacrifice? She had heard of battlefield bravery, Marines throwing themselves on grenades to save others around them. And Jesus. One of her friends had given his Grateful Dead tickets to an auction to benefit poor people. But self-centered Dad doing self-sacrifice at the cost of his whole life's work? And yet, only self-sacrifice explained all the unexplainables. She wrenched it all around into a conclusion: He sacrificed his position to cover my wrong-doing and keep me from losing whatever reputation and potential for employment I have. Her father had resigned to save her skin. He sacrificed himself for me.

Over the next three days Reb lived in a sort of daze, sleeping long hours, eating fitfully. Guilt seeped into her conscience like dew into laminated wood. Rot began, spread slowly, degrading the grain, making moral punk, causing psychic pain.

* * * * *

Nonnie wrote Phil in Vietnam. She told him about the early morning call from Frank, about Reb's framing her father. She told him that, since Frank had resigned without protest, he had evidently chosen to protect his daughter.

"But Phil," wrote Nonnie, "an interesting logical gap sits in this story that no one has mentioned, and I certainly won't. Frank says he had only two choices: either finger Reb with documented evidence that she did it, thus establishing his own innocence; or take the blame himself to protect Reb. That's not true. He had a third choice. He could have proven that the handwriting in those appointment books did not come from his hand. That's all he needed to establish his own innocence. He did not have to go so far as to match it with Reb's handwriting. He could have gone to his staff with an expert affidavit that those notations were not his handwriting. He could have said that he did not know who did and that the case is closed. Now move on. His staff would have bought that.

"That way, Reb would have caused nothing but a transient stink that Frank ventilated in one deft forensic stroke, leaving her name out of it altogether. Her malicious plot would have had no lasting effect. However, the way Frank did play it, Reb got just what she wanted: Frank humiliated and torn from his beloved firm, his life work, his fulfillment. She seems to have gotten her revenge.

"Not credible. Street-smart Frank, beat-the-system Frank took the hard way out and confessed to what he didn't do? Why? Why resign when he didn't have to? Can you, without assistance from a hallucinogen, imagine Frank Grant choosing altruism over self-interest? But the case points to that. It resembles a martyrdom, a self-giving for a higher principle. Why? What was in it for Frank? He never did anything without measurable self-gain. You Christian types have always been into self-immolation or some damn thing like that. What do you make of it, young minister? Love, Nonnie."

Phil wrote back. "Too busy to answer in detail. But when you ended your letter with 'Love, Nonnie,' I figured you were just answering your own question, not expressing any affection for me. Love, Phil."

Nonnie wrote back. "I always took you for a wise guy, Phil, but sometimes you sound like a guy who is wise. Love, Nonnie.

* * * * *

Nonnie discovered that writing to Phil helped her grieve for Lilly-Belle. She felt a little better each time. About a year after Frank resigned, Nonnie wrote Phil that she had had several talks with Frank. "He's different, Phil. This new, new Frank is different. He did an amazing reversal of attitude after he left the firm. Like a horse unhitched from the plow, he spent time at Reprise doing not much till his accountant called one day and told him he was down to his last thousand bucks and what next?

"Poor guy had never thought about cash for the many years since the firm started raking in big money. Phil, he was so smart about company money and so dumb about personal. For all those flush years, he simply told his accountant to draw money from the firm's cash reserves, enough to keep his personal bank balance over ten thousand at all times. And he never built up any personal wealth, no retirement, no savings, nothing. Lots of material assets, but no investments, nothing. So after he resigned, the money ran out. No access to the firm's cash.

"Resourceful Frank set about rectifying this. He got an estate liquidator and sold off his household stuff, his cars, his boats. He took a global trip on the proceeds. Then went the house. It was in bad shape, so he didn't get top dollar, but he did well, very well.

"And he got smart. He kept out enough of the equity to buy himself a utilitarian car and a live-aboard sailboat. With most of the balance, he bought an annuity, a big one that will give him income for life. I asked him about a job. 'No job,' he said. 'No intent to get a job. Time now for my sailboat.' Phil, do you suppose he wants this sailboat to act out some sort of self-therapy, some replay of his childhood sailing without his mother's fatal accident?"

* * * * *

Reb and Nonnie lived well together on My Coffin. Nonnie got up and ate breakfast early, Reb got up and ate brunch late. Nonnie went about her various revenue-producing tasks getting up stuff to sell at the farmer's market on Saturdays. Reb biked up to the community college for her courses. Sometimes they took an independence cruise to discuss identities, life narratives, meanings, goals, choices, decisions. Both grew.

* * * * *

Nonnie got a letter from Phil with instructions to tell the others the news: "I'm returning to my old job in Alexandria and my old apartment in Bon Vivant. Okay?" The reunion festivities with Nonnie, Hal, Brad, and Emily extended over several days and evenings including one memorable cruise on My Coffin. Phil enjoyed getting to know Reb.

* * * * *

One fine day after Frank got back from his global travels and sold Reprise and acquired his guaranteed income annuity, he drove to the marina to take a second look at the twenty-seven-foot 1980 Luger Fairwinds with a name on the transom: "The Office." It had a swing keel for shoal draft sailing, a ten-horsepower inboard diesel, and cabin headroom. Built for comfort, not performance. Symbolized, he said to himself, the new, new Frank.

Frank tried to haggle the broker down from the posted price, but the broker balked. "Oh, well, fine," said the wheeling-dealing, bottom-line, break-the-competition former president of Grant International, "if you'll paint a new name on her." "Bad luck to change a vessel's name." "This name must change." He passed over a slip of paper. "Here it is: Quest. In bright green, please. I'll settle up and sail away day after tomorrow, okay?" "Sure. A hundred for the name-change. No mark-up. My cost."

* * * * *

Frank shopped for necessary gear and bought food and stuff at the grocery store. On settlement day he handed over a cashier's check, iced the cool-box, moved everything he needed aboard Quest, not very much, and cast off.

In June, Northern Virginia gets only occasional northwest winds, but this morning brought about ten to fifteen knots through the narrow channel that leads into the Potomac. As Frank and Quest approached Reprise, Frank looked at the white sails against the blue sky and cried and cried. He sailed past Reprise, but never even glanced at it.

He ran with the wind past Quantico, cut east to round the point on the Maryland side, and slid down the dogleg toward the 301 bridge. Quest sang along under the bridge right around five that afternoon, her strong Genoa pulling well, nicely formed mainsail doing its part. She tended to yaw, as most boats do off the wind, so Frank's arms had gotten quite tired by seven-thirty. He saw Cobb Island coming up on the port side. Frank to Quest: I think we'll just tuck in there for a good meal and spend the night. But Quest didn't want to do that, and kept on sailing. Frank had forgotten how sailboats get ideas about where they want to go and where they don't want to go, so he was a little off-put to find that they were past Cobb.

And then, no wind. That's the way with the northwest winds. They go to bed at night. Early. Now it was a flood tide, and Frank thought maybe they'd drift back into Cobb, but no, they just sort of lay there while the sun slipped away. I could always fire up the diesel, thought he, but where, after all, am I trying to get to? So Frank and Quest drifted along while the stars emerged and the moon arose and really, Frank decided, this was peace. Lights in houses on the shoreline combined with flashing white, red, and green buoy lights to give a mystic appearance to the river.

Around three in the morning a slight breeze picked up out of the southeast, so Frank tacked on down the river, without a lot of energy, just letting it happen. Quest performed all right for a fiberglass production boat. Clouds came in and the river got dark, very dark. A little surface mist formed. Maybe he dozed, maybe unaccustomed darkness disoriented him, maybe the wind shifted and he didn't notice. Whatever, even though the river is only four or five miles wide here, Frank could see no more shore lights, and could see navigation lights only up close. He simply had no idea where he was. The river, yes, but where? In the eastern sky a faint glow, pink clouds. More breeze. It cleared the mist. And then the cross.

St. Clement's Island lies off the Maryland shore, about three dozen acres. At the south end stands a forty-foot cross. Just the cross, white, in broad, masculine proportions. Nothing else. It loomed dead ahead. Frank's impulse grasped him. He luffed up, dropped the sails, dropped the hook, stripped to his skivvies, rigged the boarding ladder, and dove overboard. He swam the hundred yards to the island, walked across the sandy beach to the cross, and dropped to his knees. He stayed there less than a minute. He backtracked, swam back, climbed aboard, toweled down, got dressed, went below, fixed coffee, and sat on his deck, watching rising sunlight bathe the cross of St. Clement. His thoughts ran variations on "What's that all about?" and "What am I all about?"

Frank and Quest took that day, that night, and the next morning to sail back up past Mason Neck and on to Misty Cove and Nomanisan Island. My Coffin was anchored near the dock on Nomanisan. It was Sunday morning. Nonchalance was weeding her garden. She waved at him when he called her name. She shoved off in her dinghy and rowed out to meet him while he anchored and secured. Frank gave Nonchalance a steady look. She returned it. She said, "Welcome home." "Thank you, Nonnie."

Frank looked beyond her to the island. "Nonnie!" "Yes?" "Where's Meshach? And Bedlam?" "Burned them down." "You did that?" "Yep. Too much past in them. Past serves no purpose but to teach. Can't live in the past. I was living in it. Decided to live in My Coffin, my present and my future." They got to laughing over that. Nonnie climbed up into Quest. They hugged. "Nice boat," she said, "nice reprise." Frank spent the rest of the day setting in a mooring and buoy there in Misty Cove next to My Coffin. That evening they took some fish from Nonnie's nets, went ashore on Nomanisan Island, and grilled them on Shadrach.

They became so absorbed in conversation that they never noticed Reb coming down the lane on her bike and rowing out to My Coffin.

* * * * *

When Reb emerged from the lane at Misty Cove she saw a strange sailboat moored near My Coffin. As she rowed out to the houseboat in the dark, she could see Nonnie and a man sitting near the fire in Shadrach. Her father. Her autonomic system reacted, heart racing, gut wrenching. She went to bed but didn't sleep.

A little after midnight she crept topside, careful not to wake Nonnie, slipped into her dinghy, rowed ashore in quiet stealth, and biked back to the community college. She found a bench and sat there, sat the rest of the night, through the dawn till time for her English class. Today's work: *Antigone*. Once again, she thought, her literary studies would illuminate her life. She walked to her classroom.

The professor opened with remarks on Antigone's tragic conflict. Reb felt herself drawn to this ancient woman, like herself a strong, pragmatic daughter standing up to a pig-headed, prideful father. Now Reb is motioning for a turn to speak. She's telling the class of her own experience, how her own father's arrogance has robbed her of challenge. She is just getting warmed to her insight and then she is hearing the professor say, "Thank you, Ms. McFinn. That helps us see how Antigone and Creon are indeed universal characters." Reb is tuning out.

When the class broke up, the professor said, "Ms. McFinn, come to my office please." She said, "Rebecca, I'm glad you let Antigone illuminate your life. Want to tell me the rest of the story?" Reb blurted it out, all about how his self-centeredness took him round the bend, drinking and doing self-righteous church, and how he cruelly prolonged her mother's pain, how she left home, changed her name, and renounced any inheritance. How someone revealed to her father's company that he had lived a secret life of under-the-table deals. How he had disgraced his business ethics, betrayed his employees. How she couldn't stomach him any more. How she had to get distance from him.

The professor leaned toward Reb. "That's quite a story, Rebecca. But full of holes. An incomplete narrative. It does help me understand why you walk so slumped over." She looked up into the woman's eyes. "Do what?" "You look like you're carrying a forty-pound sack of dog food."

Reb delayed her answer. "I don't understand." "Your guilt." "I have no guilt. I resent my father. I resent his manipulation." The professor's eyebrows arched. Reb said, "The way he got the upper hand by that 'sacrifice.' Just another Judas." Higher arches. "You know, dark doings at night, and betrayal." "Betrayal?" "Yes. He betrayed me after the revelation of his sleazy dealings."

The professor said, "Is that what your narrative is really all about? Something is missing. Some emotional burden that weighs you down. I hear guilt. When are you going to forgive yourself so that you can forgive him?" "I can't. Not till he . . . ." She stopped. "He what?" "Nothing. I just can't." "Rebecca, what did you do to him?" Long pause. "Nothing." "Except?"

Her emotional mast, rotten with guilt, collapsed. She broke down. The professor waited. Reb told the rest of the story. And then she said, "Okay, he figured out that I did it. I made that easy for him. But he did not choose to prove to his employees that I did it. He could have, through handwriting. Through the age of the ink. Could have sworn out a trespassing complaint. I knew all that beforehand. I wanted to see him stoop so low as to wreck his own daughter's life to avoid wrecking his own. I could endure that. I thought he would do that to me.

"I certainly didn't think he would give up without a fight. But he did resign his precious position. He left in disgrace. He went broke. He gave up everything. What possible benefit to Frank Grant came from that?" A long pause. "Self-sacrifice. Where does it come from? Why would anyone do it?" More silence. The professor said, "Nobody knows. Don't believe anyone who claims to know." Reb: "My dad protected me." "Indeed he did." "That cost him a lot." "Indeed it did." "Wow."

The professor let that sit there. Then, "Reb, take the word 'nonetheless' and put it into the right place in these sentences: 'My father said to himself, my daughter betrayed me. I want to keep my position. I must protect my daughter.'"

Reb contemplated that, then said, one word at a time, "My father said to himself, my daughter betrayed me. I want to keep my position. Nonetheless, I must protect my daughter."

She sat there, staring through the window. She said, "I'm going home now." "And?" "Change the narrative of my life." "Yes. Before you go, consider this. You have a strong intellect. In our classes we have discussed the spiritual power of the mythic, the mystic, the mysterious. You have acknowledged the existence of things ineffable and transcendent. You have discovered the abrasive power of guilt. We have seen characters for whom forgiveness has relieved guilt."

"Forgive?" Reb looked shocked. "I can never forget this." "Did I say anything about forgetting? I'm talking about transforming, a mystical work of your spirit." "Oh." "So here's your homework: If you can accept that you are moving toward a new life beyond this burden of guilt, maybe you would consider the word 'reconciliation.' Work it out, Rebecca, work out how it might apply here. That's it. Go home, young woman."

* * * * *

At Shadrach Frank and Nonnie feasted on the fish and discussed Frank's new conditions. Many months ago, he told her, he faced the death of his old dream for Grant International. He told her of his new dream conceived and birthed and now grown-up reality: his dream to live in Misty Cove, free to quest the deepest yearnings of his mind. "For this much," said Frank, "has come to clarity: in all those years since my mother died right out there on that river, I have suppressed the questions that would give her death meaning. Why did she die? I know how. But why? For what purpose? And when Lilly-Belle died, I suppressed the same questions. And when Reb did that unspeakable thing to me, her own father, why? Any meaning to be had? Or just the indifferent workings of an indifferent system?"

"Well," Nonnie told him, "I'd go with the indifferent system. Things happen through mere mechanical causes, and you'll find no grand metaphysical purposes. That explains it all for me."

Okay, he said to himself, that may be the whole story for this wonderful woman, but not for me. Here am I, I have my questions. Tomorrow I get to work on them. First stop, subdue the past, as Nonnie burned Meshach. Second stop, Phil.

At dawn Frank rowed his dinghy to the Nomanisan dock, stood on the end, recalled a few wedding words, imagined a bottle of Ripple, walked up to Quander Road and spoke to his memory of the foreman, returned, found the site of the death boat, rowed his dinghy to the channel, reenacted the flaming siege bomb and the scuttling fire, rowed back. There. Now for the future.

He walked up to Bon Vivant, found Phil, and asked him please would he come sailing some day soon to work on some hard questions. "Sail?," asked Phil. "Yeah, I think better under sail." And Phil said, "So what about right now?" Under sail a little later, Quest headed downriver toward Mt. Vernon. Sunlight sparkled on wavelets in the southwesterly breeze. Frank held a steady starboard tack.

Frank said, "Phil, my mother died right about here. The mast had rotted. Why did God let my mother die? The reverend doing the funeral said God wanted her in her heavenly home. Many years later, my wife died in excruciating pain because I followed a commandment of God that I heard from a church in Manchester. My daughter plotted a situation in my business where I had to choose between wrecking her life and wrecking my life. Why? What things came together to make those things happen? Any purpose, any meaning? The minister in that church in Manchester kept saying, 'Just have faith.' Okay, faith in what? In God? If I had enough faith, those things would not have happened?"

Phil asked whether they were going to be sailing for maybe two months so that they could find some answers. They laughed about that. On the way down to Mt. Vernon and back, he and Frank discussed these thorny issues. As they moored back in Misty Cove, Frank said, "Thanks. That helped, but about as much as a handful of peanuts instead of dinner. Appetizing, yes. Satisfying no."

* * * * *

Hal was driving back from an errand when he saw Frank walking toward Phil's garage apartment. He turned left and motored down to Nonnie's vegetable garden. "Nonnie, good morning." "And to you, Prince Hal." Hal flinched at the use of Sibyl's affectionate name. "Nonnie, what's Frank doing up in Bon Vivant?" "Dunno, but he's living on a sailboat in Misty Cove." Hal slumped. "Nonnie, that's a blow to me. What do I do?" "Hal, you go to your son and you say, 'Son, you are a self-certified horse's ass and I love you. Welcome home.'" "Nonnie, I asked you a serious question and you give me a comic answer." "Not comic, Hal, serious. If you don't like it, go figure out the wrong answer for yourself." She went back to hoeing her row of okra. Hal said, "Thank you, Nonnie."

9 First Questings

On that one amazing day, Reb encountered herself in Antigone, Frank encountered Phil's perplexing answers aboard Quest, and Hal encountered his anxiety about Frank. Not only that, but Emily and Brad encountered their lost cause.

Sitting in their sunny breakfast nook, with the same old view and the same old antique table, now over two decades more antique than it was when they first met Phil, Brad said, "and we're also more antique now, for sure." "Oh, I don't know," said Emily, "speak for yourself." "Whatever," said Brad, "and you know, the coffee spoons are long gone." "And the hollow." Emily sat back. "But Stevie will be home this time next year." Brad slumped. "I suppose you bring that up to remind me that we still have this lost cause." Emily said, "I do. Because the question has never gone away." "The question. Why? Why did Stevie do it?" "I think," said Emily, squeezing Brad's hand, "we understand his genetic defects. And we understand the temptations." The grandfather clock struck eleven times. "But what a senseless, purposeless thing. Why did this happen to such a good, decent family?"

They stared out at their trees, their landscaping. Brad: "I want to understand meaning. Understand why things happen. Find out whether anything ever happens for any lasting purpose." Emily cracked the blinds to let in some rays of sun. "Back in 1963 when we felt meaningless, Phil helped. Maybe it's time to ask him again." Brad: "Yes. But we must include Nonnie. She'll temper any over-wrought doctrines from Phil. Can't be too careful around these religious types." "Brad, that's past disrespectful. He's our friend.""He's religious. Means he has a batty streak. Unpredictable." Emily threw her damask napkin at her husband.

The doorbell. Frank. Warm greetings. Brad and Emily heard Frank's account of mooring in Misty Cove for good. "And," Frank said, "I must, must, must get some answers. My childhood in that house across the street, my parents, our sailboat, Misty Cove, Mother's death, Lilly-Belle, Reb, and so much loss. Now my new life. I must try to understand, to restore, to rebuild on new foundations."

The three, Frank in his early forties, Brad and Emily in their early sixties, so close, so far, looked into an emerging thought. Frank said, "I must find out why such things happen. I need to find purpose, if any." Brad and Emily looked at each other. Emily said, "That's a little spooky, Frank. We were just talking about meaning and purpose." Frank: "So were Phil and I. And Nonnie and I." Silence.

Emily said, "Sounds like the beginning of a group." "Group?," said Frank. Brad said, "Wonder what would happen if we got together with Phil to talk about purpose and meaning." Frank said, "Not so fast. I just came to talk to you two." "So talk." They conversed for an hour. Frank left, gratified but unsatisfied. His appetite surged.

Brad and Emily called Phil, put the case to him, asked if he would meet with them and Frank. "Sure," he said, "if you can get Nonnie in on it." When they hung up and did a high five, they went to find Nonnie. "Sure," she said. "I hope you're including Hal."

They went home by way of Hal's house and put the case to him. Hal said, "You said that Frank will be there? Do I believe that?" "We're not asking you to understand it, Hal." "Okay, I'm ready. I'm too old to dawdle. When do you want me there?"

Brad and Emily sat at their antique breakfast table. "Whew," said Brad. "What a day," said Emily.

* * * * *

Nonnie found Phil reading on his little patio. "Look, let's see whether we can get Reb to show up for that gathering at the Farriers' house. Might get her and Frank into reconciliation." Phil said, "And we might be able to demonstrate that spirituality has more to do with living your convictions than believing some doctrine."

Nonnie found Frank snoozing in the hammock rigged under Quest's boom. She said, "Frank, your daughter is living on My Coffin a few yards from you." "Too well I know that. She won't even look my way." "She's embarrassed." "So?" "So come over for breakfast tomorrow morning. Reb will be there. And your father." "My father? Why?" "Your father. Because I can invite anybody I want aboard My Coffin."

The next morning Frank rowed over and climbed aboard the houseboat. He saw his father. His father saw him. "Hello." "Hello."

Reb said, speaking an obvious script, "Hi, Dad." Frank said, "Hi, Reb." "Orange juice?" "Thanks." "Without champagne or without Ripple?" Frank examined his daughter's face, caught the hint of a grin.

Phil said, "Nonnie and I have asked the three of you to come together this morning to start a long process of reconciliation. To be blunt, you are unequipped to do it yourselves. We don't think we can make your alienation any worse, so we're gambling that we could make it better."

Reb, Hal, and Frank looked shocked. Nonnie said, "It's a long process, in stages. First you get face to face, like this, and talk about neutral matters. Later you lay out your cases. At some time you will know that you're ready to reconcile." The three sat speechless.

"So," said Phil, "Reb, what are you studying these days?" Her answer had a stilted quality. Nonnie prompted Frank to get into the conversation. Also stilted. Phil asked Hal a leading question. Strained answer. During the scrambled eggs things loosened up a bit.

After a while Phil said, "Each of you has deep grievances with each of the others. It has alienated you from one another for a long time. Of course it did. You caused great pain over these many years. That will not go away over orange juice and eggs." The toxic trio looked into the distance in three different directions.

Nonnie said, "We have, however, heard each of you yearning for reconciliation. So we want to at least get you connected. Nothing more than that for now. No need to confront your issues just yet. That will come. Stay cool."

Phil said, "Reb, your father and Brad and Emily Farrier have invited Nonnie, Hal, and me, to get together with them to discuss how and why things happen. Reasons and purposes. Nonnie and I think you could get a lot out of being there." Nonnie helped Reb see that she could do again what she had done so well in her high school discussions. Reb, strengthened from her Antigone breakthrough, looked them over and said, "Never since my mother died have I considered being in the same room with my father. But today, yes, I'll do it."

Frank spoke up. "This gives me the shakes. I still lack confidence in my conscience and judgment. I lived years to serve my own purposes at the expense of others. I want to be reconciled with my father and my daughter, but only at my pace."

Hal said, "I have felt estranged from you, Frank, for so very long. I like the idea of being around other people to buffer my anger."

* * * * *

That night Frank told himself that he felt closer to his daughter. But nowhere near reconciled. And over in My Coffin, Reb told herself that maybe, maybe she could, maybe, someday, forgive that stupid man.

* * * * *

A week later these seven characters gathered in Brad and Emily's living room. From one corner Frank watched his daughter move with young confidence. From another corner, Hal watched his granddaughter's young face, its nimbus of misuse. Brad rapped on a glass. "Thanks for coming," he said. Some smiles. Emily said, "You've each said that you have issues about how and why things happen. Some about relationships. Some about the past. Some about God. Some about meaninglessness. Some about emptiness. At least one person, all of the above." "That would be me," said Brad, trying to clown. No response. Emily said, "You've all said you seek purpose in your life. You wonder whether there's any meaning. So here we are." She pointed at Nonnie and Phil. "Thanks to you two for agreeing to help us." Nonnie took a deep drag on her cheroot, blew a noxious cloud toward Phil, and said, "Any help I give will be to bust this guy senseless if he spouts pious nonsense." Phil said, "Now, what's up? Or down?"

Hal turned from his window. "Folks," he said, "I've known you all a long time. I trust you. I have been stuffing this question for many years. Now here it comes.

"When Sibyl was growing up the ministers told her that God damns people who don't go to church. She thought that was so preposterous she stopped going to church. And of course she got scared of dying since she would go to hell."

He stared out the window down toward the river. "She died fearing God, fearing what God would do to her when she died. If I'm going to get anything out of these meetings with you, Phil, you'll have to answer big questions that have tormented me for two decades. Is there a God? Why does God do these frightful things? Where is my Sibyl? Is she or isn't she in hell?"

In the silence, Phil joined Hal. "I can not imagine how awful this has been for you. I am angry that our culture has fed you, and all the rest of you, and me too, such juvenile and superstitious ideas. I salute you, Hal, for asking these questions. I hope to help you find answers in mature ideas about a mature concept of God. But before I can do that, I must take you through some preliminaries. Must take God 101 before God 102." He turned to the others. "When we have done this we'll be ready to tackle the knotty quandaries in How? What causes thing to happen? And Why? For what purposes, if any? He turned back to Hal. "Hal, I want to answer your question. I have no pat answers. I have struggled to build answers. Can we agree to defer your question till we have done background?" "Sure. For a while."

"So." Phil turned back to the others. "Causes. Multiple choices: One, nothing: it's all causeless. Two, nature: natural laws like gravity or natural mechanisms like pathogens of illness. Three, fate: a prearranged destiny for each person. Four, astrology: the alignment of planets. Five, deity: a supernatural divinity, or God.

"You get to choose one of these causes or make up your own. I don't care, so long as you're satisfied. I have done this myself. I eliminated the first four, leaving God. But the concept of a causative God that I developed does not resemble the conventional concept of God out there in the culture, not even a little bit. But that's enough from me. Time to hear your own quandaries, your dissatisfactions and satisfactions. Please recall your images of God and let's hear about them."

Voices began, "I heard that God's a stern old man in heaven, a king and judge with flowing white hair and beard. He's sitting on a throne with Jesus on his right hand." "He hears our prayers and sometimes he does and sometimes he doesn't do what we ask." "Like the little boy who said his prayers: 'Thank you for my new baby sister. But what I asked for was a bicycle.'" "He's issuing judgments like 'Reward this guy with success,' or 'Punish that woman for her misdeeds,' or 'Let the baby get well but not the mommy,' or 'Call them both to their heavenly home.'"

Reb said, "Phil, I have heard pop evangelists talk about an angry God ready to condemn me for my sins and disbelief. St. Peter stands at the pearly gates taking names and keeping score and sending miscreants to a nether-world to toast their tootsies forevermore." Someone else said, "Religion uses threats of hell and inducements to heaven to manipulate behavior."

Brad said, "I laugh at the childishness of these notions. If that's the best religion can do, who needs it." General nodding and chuckles, including Phil's. "Well might you laugh at them. I laugh at them except when I cry over the harm they do. Two problems: they visualize God as a person, which suggests the same limitations and personality types as people. And they encourage thinking of God as an authoritarian parent running children's lives. Both problems keep people spiritual juveniles." He gulped coffee.

Emily said, "I hear about God from ministers in church, at funerals and at weddings. The one in the prayers about 'just give us this, or just fix that, or just prevent such and such.'" Brad said, "She means the God you ask to just get me a parking space, quick, before I'm late for lunch. I'll pay you on Sunday." Phil said, "I know that one. It's a little utilitarian, step-and-fetch-it godlet serving us, doing our bidding. It resembles primitive superstition and magic. It reduces God to a domesticated fixer that we can ask to intervene to get things to come out our way. It deserves about as much respect as astrology or black cats or palm reading or tea leaves or tarot cards or witch doctors or rain gods that live in volcanos."

Reb said, "I've collected some other stupid ideas about the word God: 'Act of God,' meaning hail, windstorm, flood. 'Word of God,' meaning that every word, sentence, story, and prohibition in the Bible is applicable as written. 'Wrath of God,' meaning the one third of a schizophrenic God who can't decide whether to be wrathful or loving or just."

"Phil," said Hal, "I was talking to my doctor the other day. He was saying that he works hard to heal illness in mind, body, and spirit. But he sees nothing suggesting that God wants to heal. He said that, to the contrary, he has to keep fixing stuff that God lets go wrong in bodies and minds and spirits. He said that he even worries that God has built a propensity for illness into the bodily system."

Frank said, "No matter how great your explanations, Phil, I'll not believe in this loving, all-knowing, all-powerful God we hear about who let the Nazis incinerate millions of Jews. Or, worst of all, that God actually used the Nazis to punish them. For not being Christians? In fact, I'll not believe in any God that would do any of the rotten things that go on. Or condone the injustice in this world. How can we believe that God is just when evil people succeed just fine and good people get destroyed?"

Nonnie said, "Let me read you this card I found. It has a little ditty by someone named Charles Synge Christopher Bowen. It says 'The rain it raineth on the just, and also on the unjust fella; but chiefly on the just, because the unjust steals the just's umbrella.'"

"And these churches," Emily said, "I am disgusted with the church that has sponsored the cruel Crusades, the monstrous Inquisition, the bloody wars between Catholics and Protestants, and so forth."

Phil said, "Folks, I too do not believe that God does those rotten things, or promotes those things, or allows those things, or is punishing anybody. Much to the contrary. I think God grieves the pain and suffering in the world." Silence, but all eyes were on Phil.

Reb said, "I was wondering why if God knows everything before it happens we should pray, since nothing will change no matter what." Phil said, "Well, why must you assume that God knows everything? We can't be certain about the concept of time, let alone God's function in time. But whatever, consider other questions. Would God know our future because it is already fixed, predetermined? Or does God treat us like puppets, deciding our future minute by minute? Or is our future unknowable because it is constantly developing, unfolding according to the choices we make and the things that happen to us?"

He waited for a response. None. He continued. "If the future is fixed, why bother to do anything about it? If it's contingent, you are responsible for managing it as best you can. Each view implies a certain concept of God: either God specifies your future, or God walks with you into your future. Which one you choose determines what you do about your life."

Reb said, "I have spiritual hunger but no appetite for church. I do get fed when Grandma Nonnie talks about the spirituality of nature. She finds God in the beauty and honesty of the natural world, in homeostasis, synergism. The natural world sustains us, but we exploit it. If God created all this, why doesn't God protect it? How come we get away with killing the golden goose, this planet? Anyhow, the little I know about God does intrigue me. If you can fill me in on that without damaging Nonnie's ideas about the sacredness of nature, I'll listen."

"Phil?" It was Nonnie. "As Reb said, I believe in nature, and also in simplicity, individualism, self-sufficiency. I don't do Christianity in any of its forms. I believe in love, in nurture, in generosity, and in hospitality. I find sacred truth in the wild places, the water, the green growth, the air, the rich earth, the life abundant in the natural world. Why would I want your God, transcendent or immanent?"

"Beautiful images, Nonnie." Phil paused, continued. "I can't answer your question. You have your own spirituality of the sacred and the spiritual capacity to appreciate it."

Reb said, "Religion can get involved in public policy questions. In our modern history and government class we're studying the conflict between science and religion. Some extreme scientists say that scientific naturalism and determinism alone can explain how the world came to be, fourteen billion years ago. Therefore some scientists become atheists, hostile to religion, which they consider an irrationality that has damaged civilization.

"On the other side, extreme fundamentalists adopt creationism, which says the Bible explains how the world started six thousand years ago. For them, that invalidates scientific explanations and the atheism that science encourages. Atheism, they continue, causes immorality and the decline of civilization. So, according to these two extremes, science is causing immoral atheists, and religion is causing irrational biblicists.

"The creationists promote a simple remedy: a contrivance called 'intelligent design' that repackages creationism in pseudo-science. They push school boards to include this in the biology curriculum to correct alleged errors in the theory of evolution. It's spreading enough to dilute science education nationwide. Of course scientists and others concerned for the advancement of science and technology resist this incursion. It has become a First Amendment issue of the separation of religion and state."

Phil said, "I'm trying to articulate a theology that integrates biblical theology and scientific insights into a single statement that honors both disciplines equally, diminishing neither. Lets science say how stuff happens and religion say why. Seems simple enough. But it threatens extremists."

Brad fiddled with his pipe. "I majored in physics, and I know what causes what in this universe. I was taught that scientific naturalism explains everything. The universe began with natural law. Science explains the endless chain of causes and effects. It explains evolution. There's only one question: How? And only one source of the answer: Science. Whodunnit? Nature dunnit, and natural law enforces it. Period.

"If you accept that, you do not need something in your imaginations called God." He looked at Phil to see the reaction. None observable. "I believe in material, measurable, observable data, and I believe in what you can know from studying this reality."

Emily said, "We have a friend who is one of the creationists Reb discussed. He goes to a church that's the real deal, he says, because they take the Bible seriously. He says that the Bible is the word of God and therefore when it says that God created the world in six days, it means just that and the scientists are wrong."

"Well," said Brad, "I think that this question of purpose, the Why?, has no answer. I think that science answers the question, 'How.' And God? If you're trying to name the ultimate, the supreme, the first cause, the name is not God, but natural law." In the silence, he took a deep draw on his pipe and continued. "Soon after I graduated, I talked to a churchy guy who said you can't believe in God and also believe in science. So I chose to believe in science and forget religion. And I'm not giving up science."

Phil said, "And why should you? I would never suggest you do. Your churchy guy was flat wrong. Sound science and sound religion do not contradict each other. They supplement each other. In fact, I think that you cannot get coherent answers unless you include them both. I'll show you how. If you respect data, analysis, and logic, stay with my reasoning and I will lead you, through both science and the Bible, to a rational concept of God and a reliable spirituality. With those, you can find satisfying answers to How? and Why?"

Emily said, "So, Phil, what about you and your ideas about

God?" Phil took his time, examining the inside of his coffee cup. He looked up. "At one point I had nothing but my small and narrow humanism. I had rational convictions rooted in my social conscience. I had intellectual dedication to justice. Over time I realized that these roots were subsisting on shallow, parched soil. No spiritual nourishment. Plenty of head-trips, cognitive understandings, but no connections to my heart. I had no spiritual companion. Oh, I had friends. We shared thoughts and dreams. I mean I had no God above and beyond my head. I had no God in my heart. So I framed an hypothesis: maybe God is a reality, not a figment.

"My yearning for a connection above and a connection within activated my hidden spiritual side. I began to seek a concept of God. Trouble was, I associated God with church, and I had the same objections to church you have raised. Also I found a confused array of concepts: A different God for Catholics, Protestants, Buddhists, Judaists, Muslims, Hindus. Various versions of God: domesticated, utilitarian, judgmental, civic, liturgical, manageable, scientific, magical, subdivided, definable. A God of prosperity, of personal salvation, of nature, of piety, of the marginalized. A God from the Old Testament, a God confined to the boundaries of Jesus, a God of patriotic nationalism. A God of dogma and doctrine. And so forth.

"I did find nourishing ideas at this vast steam table, but I also found them variously overdone, underdone, putrid, smelly, disguised, narrow, shallow, childish, arrogant, complacent, vague, implausible, and angry. And compartmentalized, exclusivist: If you don't believe such and such, you can't be one of us. So I yearned for a great aromatic pot combining the best of each concept of God into a tasty, nutritious stew.

"I began assembling my own concept. I insisted that it include both God transcendent and God immanent. God far above and beyond my comprehension. And God here and now, companionable, communicative, and involved in our lives. Both simultaneously, equally, and synergistic. I sought a broad and deep theology, one based on the Bible without being biblicist, and simultaneously based on science. I needed a boundless concept of God. I have a little book by J. B. Philips called *Your God Is Too Small.* The title alone expands my thoughts about boundless God.

"I sought God in nature and in science. God in the Bible. God in the spirituality of the church, worship, and prayer. God in service and in giving. I checked out mainline churches, charismatic, evangelical, and fundamentalist churches. Taken in moderation and with a critical eye for flim-flam, each showed some merit, but they all suffer from doctrines either too narrow, too shallow or too broad. They believe too much or too little. So, after all this struggle, I have found that I must not only know about God but know God personally as I know my friends. And as I get to know God I make regular additions and corrections to my concept. It is evolving. This requires clear thinking and lots of it. But far more than thinking, heartfelt prayer, steady Bible study, generous giving, serving human needs, policies of reconciliation, discriminating study of the traditions of the church, honest reasoning, faithful worship." "It's as easy as that?," asked Frank. He was smiling. Others laughed in an ironic tone. Phil smiled. "That easy. And now God has become my central reality."

"You know, Phil," said Hal, "when I was young I heard all this stuff about God. We all did. It's in the culture, in movies and jokes and churches and cartoons. It's all so childish, so primitive. When my Sibyl died, I needed an adult God. The minister at the funeral tried to say why she died. Said God called her home. Nonnie had to evacuate me. You gave me a scientific God, all causes and effects, gravity and rot. You explained how Sibyl died, not why. I had to tell you to leave my house. I still don't know what Sibyl died for."

"Well, Hal, I regret that. My explanation had severe limitations. It has grown since then. Again I assure you we can work together toward answers to these vexing questions. And perhaps find some reconciliation with the irreconcilable.

"I'll give you what I can. But it's like cooking. I spice to my taste. When you cook, you spice to your taste. I'll not presume to sell you my concept of God. This will be your quest. I'll offer you various choices and you choose your own and take responsibility for your own stuff. I'll open a spiritual grocery store for your personal shopping. You take whatever gives you spiritual nutrition. I hope you will decide freely on your own answers. Sorry about the mixed metaphors." Some body language showed some interest.

* * * * *

"To get started, I ask you to forget your present concepts of God. Please make a blank slate. Dump all the conventional, popularized concepts of God that you have absorbed from the culture. Dump whatever notions you've gotten from movies, children's books, cartoons, jokes, great paintings, conversations, Bible stories, churches. Dump everything you've ever heard about God. Forget it all.

"I'll help you replace all that with a concept of God that will offer reasonable explanations for why things happen and what God has to do with what happens. I think it offers love, not threat."

Nonnie said, "Phil, I respect you, but you seem obsessed with contriving some grand theology. Not helpful in the realities of life. Here's another little ditty for you. I don't know who wrote it, but it tells the truth about what happens when hard tragedy confronts abstract explanations. 'Your logic my friend, is impeccable. Your theology undoubtedly true. But since the dirt fell on the coffin, I keep hearing that and not you.'

"So, my friend, I say that the only doctrine you need says love your neighbors and do to them what you would want them to do to you. It's called the golden rule. Every religion has adopted it. It's universal and it's true and it works. Why all this fuss over God?"

* * * * *

Two mornings later, Nonnie and Phil pulled off another breakfast conference with their estranged trinity. While Nonnie broke eggs for the omelet, Phil said, "You all survived that first gathering, right?" Nods. "Nonnie and I are raising the ante." Suspicion. They explained their new plan. By the time Nonnie served the omelet, Frank, Reb, and Hal sat in thoughtful silence. Phil and Nonnie finished their pitch while the omelet went cold. An hour later, however, the three of them left in a provisional detente, united in a scheme both frightening and exhilarating. But not, not, not reconciled. Far too much pride at stake on all three sides. Hal walked to Bon Vivant. Reb pedaled up the lane. Frank sailed downriver, didn't come back for three days.

10 Cosmic Causes of What Happens

On the next appointed evening, Brad and Emily welcomed their questers to a second session. Phil said, "Right. Last month we heard your concerns and issues. Hal got us started with the question that haunts us all: Why did that awful thing happen to Sibyl? Let's confront it head on. It's everyone's question. But I want to divide it into two manageable parts. First, how do things happen? Anything. Good, bad, anything at all. How? Second, for what purpose, if any, do things happen, good, bad, anything at all? Why? To what intended outcome? This is a question of meaning. What does anything that happens mean? If anything."

Nonnie said, "Too many words, Phil, as usual. If you had to pay five dollars a word, you would have said, first, what causes stuff? How? Second, for what reason? Why?"

Phil said, "Thanks. Last time Brad told us, and I quote, 'I majored in physics, and I know what causes what in this universe.' So I've asked him to teach us a quick lesson on how things work."

"Hang on, people," said Brad, "we're going cosmic. First, come with me back fourteen billion years ago. Nothing there except the Big Bang. This colossal expansion starting causing happenings. The very first happenings were time, and space and matter and gravity and energy and the laws of science that govern how everything works. Every one of these happenings caused many new happenings. Since then, this universe of happenings has been expanding more and more, causing everything that has ever happened and that ever will happen."

Brad's explanation led to an outburst of associations: "Is the Big

Bang the same as the First Cause?" "Is that also called the Kalam Cosmological Principle?" "Didn't deism come from that idea?" "That's just determinism, isn't it?" Brad said, "Sounds like I just caused another happening."

Reb said, "We learned all that in school. But I never thought it would connect with my grandmother's death that Hal asked about."

"Well," said Phil, "it does. Hal?" Hal stood and said, "I've braced myself for this. It comes hard. Sibyl and I decided to replace the mast on Windermere. I went and bought strips for the lamination. She asked me, and I remember her exact words, 'I thought you were going to get these strips in white cedar. This looks like spruce.' Why do you suppose that sentence haunts me? I'll answer that in a minute. She and I and Frank glued and screwed those strips, shaped them, and varnished them. Somehow a hairline crack opened between the laminates. Water got in, with bacteria, which began the rotting. Here's my nightmare: spruce. White cedar resists rot. When the lumber mill didn't have white cedar, I didn't want to waste time shopping for better wood. I bought strips that would in time cause my own wife's death."

Dead silence. Then Frank: "Father, here's my nightmare. When Lilly-Belle and I were just nine and twelve, we took Windermere out for a sail. I remember one violent flying jibe. The boom crashed over and must have caused the mast a wrenching torque. Probably tore open that hairline crack. And you and Mother had told me not to go sailing alone. I rationalized. I wasn't alone, I was with Lilly-Belle."

Nonnie: "I was watching you two kids sailing. I could have stopped you, but I think kids need freedom to make mistakes. Had no idea this mistake would open up a fatal crack in the mast."

Hal said, "Phil, after Sibyl died, I asked you why she died and you took me through all those causes and effects. I'm an engineer. I understood that then, I understand it now. It explains how it happened. And I can understand how all the causes from the Big Bang traced down to cause her death at that frightful moment in 1963. Meeting each other at Lake Windermere in 1944. Moving to

BonVivant with baby Frank. Sibyl's accepting Frank's invitation to go sailing. Her heading into the wind to relieve the strain. That one prudent move of good boat-handling actually sent the masthead right for the one cubic foot on this planet occupied by her skull.

"All that I understand. I still don't understand why God let this frightful, cruel, meaningless thing happen. And by the way, a month ago I asked you where Sibyl is now, in hell or not. Any answers?"

Phil started to put his arm around Hal's shoulder. Hal: "Don't patronize me." Reb went to her grandfather. Frank slumped in a chair. Phil said. "Please forgive me, Hal. I want to get to these answers, but we do have to lay some foundations before any structure of categories can support them." Nonnie said, "We're all with you, Hal, and your questions are our questions."

Hal faced the window. Waved his hand back toward the group. "Carry on. I'm okay."

Phil said, "Brad, do you have more for us?" "Yep. Sibyl died because the laws of physics determined the atmospheric and hydrologic conditions at that second in time. Fixed dynamics governed the speed of that particular wind, the strength of that rotten mast at that time, and the pull of gravity as influenced by the centrifugal force set up when Sibyl turned hard into the wind.

"Given those values in those conditions, that masthead would have intersected with Sibyl's head one million times in every one million iterations. At that moment under those conditions, that lethal blow was going to happen, guaranteed. The laws are consistent. No margin for variation." He looked around. Some confusion, some lightbulbs.

Hal said, "I have just realized something. I hate those laws for doing what they did to my wife. They did not care what they were doing. They did what they do every time. The combination at that time and place killed Sibyl. That part I can get. Here's my new thought.

"As an engineer, I use the reliability of those laws to calculate strengths, weight-bearing, resistance, and durability. I can design a structure to work because I can depend upon the laws to work.

I designed that mast to be strong enough to work reliably. It did, for nine years. I did not calculate the crack and the rot. The laws governing those worked reliably also. Horrible outcome. But for nine years, the system worked as I intended. For nine years, those laws caused good things to happen. Then the brisk wind hit the rotten mast. Those two conditions caused the bad thing."

Phil said, "Hal, you just said two important things. First, affirming the value of reliable laws. Second, affirming that those reliable laws caused not only terrible things like Sibyl's death but also very many good things. So, when you ask, How did that bad thing happen?, to be fair about it, you also must ask, How did this good thing happen? And Why? Why did both good and bad things happen?"

The questers spent a few minutes turning this thought over to see about it. Emily said, "To be really fair about it, consider how many good things are happening right now. Everybody's autonomic system is working, the roof isn't leaking in this downpour outside, we had enough to eat today, no one in our families got run over. All good things. In the big picture, perhaps more good things than bad things all the time." "Sure," said Phil, "that's true in this country, but in the third world the margin comes out pretty slim. Nonetheless, I agree with your point, Emily. Good stuff is everywhere. But bad stuff gets more attention."

Brad said, "One more piece of science to supplement our understanding of deterministic outcomes, these rigid causes and effects. Called uncertainty. Back in the mid-1920s, a scientist named Heisenberg was working in a new field called quantum physics. He discovered that subatomic particles did not behave with predictable reliability. His discovery has the name Heisenberg Uncertainty Principle. Otherwise reliable physical laws have a tiny loophole where unpredictable things can happen, where they lose reliability. Very tiny loophole. I don't know what that means. It simply sits there as a fact of science. Like that well-trained, well-behaved dog we had who was walking through the living room, a little groggy and preoccupied, and absent-mindedly lifted his leg on the Christmas tree. Totally out of character and unexpected. Surprised him and us. Like a quark with a mind of its own."

After a bit of laughter, Phil said, "File the question of uncertainty for later. It may tell us what mechanism God uses to make non-scientific things happen. Okay, that's it for tonight. We've established a baseline answer to the first question: How things happen, good things and bad things. They happen in fixed obedience to laws of science originated in the Big Bang. Almost fourteen billion years later they are still causing happenings as we speak. Except, according to brother Heisenberg, when they don't."

* * * * *

At the next gathering, Phil said, "We're asking How? and Why? Last time we got a grip on the How question: how things happen in a universe governed, within perhaps uncertain boundaries, by reliable natural laws. These natural laws originated in the Big Bang. And the origin of the Big Bang? Some say, Nothing, it just happened. Others say, deity, or God.

"Brad, I think you prefer the first solution, that nothing at all originated the Big Bang." "Yep," said Brad, "nature takes care of itself. No deity needed. So I am an informed atheist by choice. But I respect those who go the other way."

Phil said, "That's mutual. And I do agree, the Big Bang is the First Cause. But I'm uncomfortable with your spontaneous, causeless Big Bang. We live in our tangible universe of time and space and matter and natural law and so forth. I perceive also another domain, not tangible. It's a domain beyond the tangible. It transcends all time and all space and all matter. So we call it transcendence. It's infinite eternity, boundless and timeless. I think that the tangible Big Bang originated from intangible transcendence. But I prefer to use an additional term for transcendence. I choose to speak of transcendent God. Transcendent God originated the Big Bang. And therefore we can say that God created all that is. Just what, by the way, the Bible says. Science and Bible, hand in hand."

Hal said, "Am I finally getting an answer, Phil? God is responsible for the causes and effects that led to my Sibyl's death?" Phil said, "That is, yes, one conclusion if you prefer to stop there. We have more to do to get to an expanded conclusion." "Phil," said Hal, "this is long and tiresome and frustrating." "Amen," said a chorus.

Emily said, "I'm thinking that this first cause, the Big Bang, may have originated another sort of result. Over four billion years ago, all that causality produced this planet, and within another billion or so years, life emerged from the chemistry. So far, the dynamic has been developmental, cumulative, causes causing causes, each accumulating more universe, more features, more structures, more dynamics. Or, to use a term from biology, our universe appears evolutionary."

Brad said, "Yes, and when life did emerge, it began to evolve until we got to humankind. And a new feature evolved: abstractions, concepts, emotions, psychology, love, hate, anger, affection, loyalty and so forth. The numberless intangibles that humans work with. Language, thought, feelings. Relationships. Every one of those is the result of a cause that stems from that first cause, the Big Bang."

Emily said to Brad, "And you, Mr. Informed Atheist, just made my case. Where did those intangibles originate? From transcendence, from God. God provided the potentials for those to emerge as conditions became right for them, when humankind evolved."

Phil said, "Many thanks, Emily and Brad. May I combine your views into one sentence on the easel: (A) How do things happen? According to God's fixed laws of physics, chemistry, and biology: predictable effects of naturalistic causes."

Reb said, "Since we are being analytical about the causes and consequences of my grandmother's death, I'll note that it indirectly caused my own birth. Am I supposed to rejoice or grieve?" That enigma sparked a general discussion that lasted late.

* * * * *

In the weeks before the next meeting, Phil and Nonnie met with their strained triad several times to rehearse their scheme.

In time, Hal, Frank, and Reb enriched their detente. They found paradoxical pleasure in collaborating on their bold strategy that could, Phil and Nonnie assured them, be both therapeutic and instructional. Like prisoners who despise one another's crimes while insisting on their own innocence, each found enough tolerance to tunnel together out of their animosity. But no reconciliation. No way. Not yet.

* * * * *

At the next gathering, Phil said, "Let's review." He read from the easel what he had written: "(A) How do things happen? According to God's fixed laws of physics, chemistry, and biology: predictable effects of naturalistic causes." And he wrote an additional clause: "which originated from God transcendent, out there, beyond."

"Objection," said Brad and Nonnie in unison. Nonnie said, "Beyond the scope of evidence." Reb said, "Not, however, beyond the scope of logic. Look, both of you have displayed strong evidence of love for others, for empathy, for justice and fairness, for other intangibles. Where did all that come from? Materialistic, mechanistic transactions? Don't think so. I think something transcendent brings that intangible stuff into being."

"Okay, Reb," said Brad, "I take your point. But the word God carries so much negative baggage that I cannot accept it. Transcendence, yes." Nonnie said, "Yes. I also accept the deep reality of the intangibles. But transcendence, no. Put me down for sacred nature."

Emily said, "I'm with Reb. I did some reading: seems that thinking the Big Bang just happened with no cause is called scientific naturalism. Thinking that transcendent God originated the Big Bang is called scientific theism. But neither one satisfies me. Regardless of whether God did or did not originate this mechanistic universe, I cannot accept the idea that we live where nothing has meaning, nothing cares for us and our lives. I need more."

11 Questing through Biblical Parallels

"Well," said Phil, "Transcendence names only one facet of God, the utterly other, the beyond beyond, part A. Consider part B, a different facet: God here and now, God immanent. Immanence means present among us, local, concerned, interactive. The opposite of transcendent. No concept of God that neglects either of these can be complete. So." He wrote on the easel, "(B) God immanent, God right here, interactive."

"What data will disclose this facet of God? The Bible. In the Old Testament God has a distinct personality, right here, right now, present, communicative. God, invisible, speaks, responds, makes decisions, and causes this and that to happen. Farther along, in the New Testament, God speaks, responds, makes decisions, and causes this and that to happen also. But visible, in the flesh and blood of Jesus, here and now, human, in action. Throughout the Bible, then, whether invisible or visible, God has immanence, interactive presence among us.

"Now we have God beyond, transcendent, and God here, immanent. Both causing, making things happen. Through actions that are both fixed and flexible." He wrote on the easel, "A + B = C, providence." He said, "I'll talk about the meaning of the term providence later. I just want you to see where we are headed. For now, let's get into the Bible's picture of God immanent.

"First, does anyone think that the Old Testament shows a wrathful and judgmental God and the New Testament a loving and forgiving God?" Some hands waved. "That's usual. And, excuse me, mistaken. Here's why. Images of God that we get in the culture

111

from movies, children's Bible stories, jokes, and so forth do show God wrathful. Those impressions stick. But they are misleading, not at all the accurate picture.

"So I read the whole Bible, from Genesis to Revelation. I discovered that the Bible is a unit, like a novel or a play or a history, with continuity from beginning to end. It tells one story and portrays one God. Only the Bible taken as a whole can disclose the complete picture of God and God's policies, God immanent, here among us, working with us and for us.

"At this point we could read the Bible to see this firsthand. Or I could summarize the Bible for you. But no, we'll discover the plot of the Bible by seeing how one person's life parallels the plot of the Bible. Frank, are you still up for this?"

Frank said, "Just barely. Very hard to do. But on balance I think so." Deep breath. "Okay. Phil and Nonnie have had long conversations with me, Reb, and Hal. They have been trying to restore our trust in one another after these twenty-some years of alienation. Hard going. We are bitter at one another. But we're better than we were. Bitter but better. We have not gotten to reconciliation. We may never. These sessions are helping.

"Phil and Nonnie have spent hours with us, sometimes together, sometimes individually. We have reflected on our lives to find meaning and purpose. We've asked how and why it all happens. Now we're ready to bring our thoughts together to see what conclusions might emerge. Feels risky. But worth a try if we all agree to it."

Reb said, "I never thought I'd hear myself agree with anything this man ever said, and definitely not in public, but I say ditto." She looked around the circle of kind faces. "I've got a lot to learn. I've got to grow up some time." Hal held up his hand and said, "Concur." Brad and Emily nodded assent.

Frank said, "We used Phil's idea that the Bible has a plot which our lives parallel. So, Phil will give you a phase in the biblical plot and I'll tell you how my life has paralleled it. The rest of you may hear your own parallels."

Phil said, "Genesis begins with a mythic account of our

beginnings. The story says that humankind started in a peaceful, stable relationship with God. Frank?" "Me too. I started life in an idyllic setting in Bon Vivant and Misty Cove. In Hal and Sibyl's happy marriage I was a beloved child."

Phil wrote on the easel, "(1) Initial equilibrium with God: a relationship of mutual trust."

"Hold it, Phil," said Emily, "did I hear you say that Genesis is a myth?" "You did, Emily. I use 'myth' as a term of respect for a traditional narrative that expresses a truth higher than a literal account could do. A myth embeds profound truths.

"Then," Phil continued, "a destabilizing event disrupted that equilibrium, causing alienation in God's relationship with humankind. The Genesis myth uses a tempting serpent to separate humankind, represented by Adam and Eve, from God. They broke trust with God, became alienated from God and from each other."

He wrote "(2) Disequilibrium: alienation from God and each other" on the easel.

Phil said, "Frank?" Frank said, "For me, the alienation had two phases. First came natural forces that caused my mother's death. Second came my irrational anger and irresponsibility that led me to cause Lilly-Belle's pregnancy, preeclampsia, and a child we were unready to support. These happenings destroyed the peaceful equilibrium in our family and alienated me from my relationships."

Brad said, "Interesting. Here's an abstraction like alienation with natural causes." "Sure," said Phil, "the Bible gives us instances of both natural and human causes for what goes wrong, as well as what goes right. Causes in the Bible, and I think in life, stem equally from natural and human sources. Nature and humankind are welded together, constantly and interactively causing stuff, good stuff, bad stuff. Genesis shows this causal unity when the natural serpent and the human representatives collude to become alienated from God." Brad looked skeptical.

"Dad," said Reb, "since we are talking down and dirty truth here, I need to get in with my own view. It does, after all, speak to how I got on this tormented earth. Only in the past month have I heard the whole sordid story of the Charlottesville caper."

Phil saw Reb scan her new friends with mixed trust and distrust. He watched them, her silent cheerleaders, support this young warrior fighting for her authenticity. She said, "In all this truth-telling. I found out that my parents did not want me, that my coming disrupted two university careers, broke a father-son bond, over-worked a grandmother-to-be. I managed, in the womb, to cause all that alienation. Good work, fetus."

A long pause. Nonnie spoke. "Sorry to interrupt. If we're gathering data, let's get it all. Lilly-Belle, bless her heart, had good sense, mostly, but her bad judgment here included going to Charlottesville at all and letting that moose juice sneak up on her. She bears some responsibility for getting herself into that pickle. No pristine, innocent victim there."

Pause. Reb spoke. "And I discovered a hard truth about my identity. I am not a child of love, but irresponsibility. I'm here not because two people planned a loving family, but because they got drunk and promiscuous."

Hal sat very still in a corner. Phil saw him flinch at these clinical accounts of the worst thing that had ever happened to him. "Frank and Reb," Hal said, "your candor refreshes, yes, but I also need full disclosure. You didn't mention my role in this. Let the record show that I too contributed to the pot of alienation that boiled over in those frightful days, nay, years. I blamed you, Frank, for varnishing over the crack in the mast that allowed rot to intrude. That was sloppy reasoning. You couldn't see the crack. Then, in my grief and anger, I slammed the door on you and Lilly-Belle. For years I nursed that wound open. As you did also."

Both Frank and Hal had to lean over so that their eye-wipes were not so public. Reb didn't care. She swabbed herself right out in the open. Nonnie sat next to her on the floor, cross-legged, arms crossed, eyes dry and kind.

The people gathered here in all this truth seemed to Phil like first-time parents in a delivery room, collaborating in God's reconciling labor to bring Reb and Frank and Hal's new relationship to birth, Nonchalance serving as midwife. Brad and Emily passed around some cookies and refilled coffee cups.

Phil said, "Ready to continue?" Some resettling. "The biblical account goes on to tell how God endured humankind's alienating behavior, starting with Adam and Eve and extending through all the Genesis myths. I would have expected God to condemn them all for their faithlessness and cut them off, terminate them. Shut off their power and water, disconnect their phone. But no, these initial disclosures show God's forgiving character and policies. Instead of punishing us as we deserved, God approached Abraham and called him to collaborate in the Israel enterprise. Not a curse, but a call. An unexpected act of acceptance. Undeserved. An act of grace."

On the easel he wrote "(3) God called Abraham." He said, "Frank, how did the call work for you? How does it resemble God's call to Abraham?"

Frank: "Okay. Here goes. I did all that alienation. Nonnie could have written me off as a soft, spoiled college kid with over-developed hormones and under-developed character. She could have set about coping with Lilly-Belle's pregnancy on her own. However, like God calling Israel to new collaboration, she hauled herself down to Charlottesville and extracted certain commitments from me. She supported Lilly-Belle and me over the next several years with tough love. She intimidated me, loved me, coached me, sympathized with me, all in measures calibrated to keep me going.

"I know now what I couldn't see then, that regardless of my alienating behavior, I received undeserved support from Nonnie, Phil, Brad, and Emily, little of which I even noticed, let alone appreciated, being self-centered. What I deserved they didn't give: rejection, write-off, condemnation, and all the other ways they could have diminished me to irrelevant. I betrayed the gift of the life my family gave me. Nonetheless, Nonnie and all remained faithful to me and called me to a responsible course of self-help. It's the first of the many nonetheless features of my story. I see it now as similar to God's call to Abraham. It has the same dynamics."

Phil: "May I point out that the unquestioning support Frank

experienced has a name. We call it grace. You can also call it undeserved love. Or nonetheless love. Or grace-love. Now, back to Abraham. God called him although the sensible thing to do would be to let humankind rot. God didn't do that, however, and invited humankind's return to communion. So Abraham, faithful Abraham, followed God's call, as did Isaac and Jacob and all the other Israelites. Some ended up in Egypt, where they fell into bondage under a cruel pharaoh called Yul Brynner." Phil looked at Frank. "Know the movie, Frank?" Laughter, for Frank had talked about how he had learned all about the ten commandments from Charlton Heston.

Frank said, "I'll let that pass for now, pal, but don't walk home alone in the dark."

"Question." Brad signaled to speak. "You are telling this story as though it happened literally as written. Do you take everything in the Bible literally like this? It says some preposterous, factually impossible things." "Thanks for reminding me. Short answer: No. Long answer: I am seeking the meaning of the Bible, what it means, what message it delivers, what deep truth it conveys. But I cannot get that meaning unless I first comprehend what it says, literally. What is its plot? Who are its characters? What themes emerge? How did it get written? Then, only then can I ask, Now, what does that mean?"

Nonnie said, "Again, too many words. Just remember ten words: First, what does it say? Second, what does it mean?"

Phil continued. "Right. Back to the story. Israel suffered this miserable existence in bondage in Egypt far from their homeland and from God, with hard labor and no freedom." On the easel appeared "(4) Israel suffered Egyptian bondage."

Frank said, "Nonnie gave us all the support of every sort that she could. But anger still corrupted my relationship with Lilly-Belle. I worked in virtual bondage as a laborer day and night. I built a company that made money but not happiness. Lilly-Belle and I inhabited a strange emotional land, far from our stable family life at Nomanisan Island and Bon Vivant.

"In this equivalent of Israel's Egypt, a pharaoh called ambition enslaved me. Ambition seeped into my moral mast and rotted my conscience. I became predatory on an old landowner, deceiving him so I could grab a huge piece of prime land on Mason Neck at a price absurdly low considering what was going to happen on Mason Neck the next year. This land let me make as much money as I wanted. A lot.

"My success made me hunger for more influence, more money, more power, more control, more material stuff. This hunger enslaved my motivation. I drove myself more than any slave driver could. Alcohol numbed the pain, but ordinary metabolism brought it right back. More alcohol, quick. Where's the freedom to live a full life under those conditions? I call that bondage. I had no real freedom." Phil watched his friends glued to this account. Frank slumped into his chair, alone. Silence, except for rain on the roof, wind swirling trees visible through the window overlooking the river. Some minutes passed.

Phil broke the silence. "First bondage, then exodus." He paused to let people return to the narrative. "The Bible says that God saw Israel's suffering in bondage, heard their cries of pain, and responded with a great act of deliverance. Called Moses to get to work for him, to lead Israel through the Red Sea and onto the Sinai peninsular." On the easel, he drew a rough outline of the Mediterranean Sea, the Nile, the Red Sea, and Sinai, tracing a route up, over, and down. He labeled it "(5) Exodus."

"So, Frank, here you come, up out of Egypt, through the Sea, and into the Sinai Peninsula. What was that like?" "Well," said Frank, "what I can remember through all that vodka haze wasn't much fun. But I don't remember making any cries of pain . . . ."

"Stop there, Dad." Reb faced him. "We went over this part. Your arrogance, defensiveness, controlling, and domineering ways expressed your cries of pain. Normal people don't do those things. You were crying out for release daily, hourly to your bottle, to your ego, to all your powers. So don't minimize this story. It's too important. Get it right."

"But Reb," said Frank, "I wasn't crying out to God." Reb said, "We talked about that. Phil said that God hears all expressions of dismay, discouragement, despair and so forth as prayers. Even the ones camouflaged as anti-social behavior express the pain of the heart. God hears pain and suffering. Even I caught on to that." During this tutorial, Frank's gaze at his daughter mixed distaste with embarrassment with amusement with pride with ironic appreciation with insight. "Great God," he said, "we don't call you Reb for nothing."

Phil: "What can I say. Frank's experience makes me watch for God's gracious acts of deliverance, disguised in clever ways, carrying us out of our various conditions of bondage into a new place." "Splendid words, Phil," said Brad, "but what was his exodus, anyhow? How did Frank get delivered?" Frank: "Coronary. Bypasses. Physical therapy, AA. I did it all. Got off the juice. Turned over a new leaf." He looked around. But that doesn't mean that I turned into a decent person. Mustn't confuse exodus with renewal.

"In our conversations about this, I discovered that my exodus event didn't lead to something any better than the bondage I had. But it did deliver me from my special bondage. I had to decide what to do with it. I didn't decide well." He saw faces wondering what he was talking about. "I think that's all I'm willing to divulge about the matter."

Phil said, "Back now to the biblical plot. We have just explored the Exodus. The next stop for the Israelites was Mt. Sinai, where God made a covenant with them. They were to be faithful to the law, centered on the ten commandments, and God would be faithful to them. God promised an unconditional covenant. A beautiful invitation to perpetual communion with God." He wrote on the easel, "(6) The unconditional covenant with God."

"How did that play out for you, Frank?" Frank said, "Well, I started going to church." "And that," said Reb, "is when you became obnoxious and sanctimonious at a cosmic level. You traded drunk on the spirits to drunk on the spirit." "Hold on, Reb," said Frank, looking defensive, "doesn't that overstate the case?"

Reb said, "No doubt you want to think so. I don't. You did give up drinking and you did take up church-going. But that particular church intoxicated you on its false covenant of rigid religiosity: obey the commandments and be saved. And they meant all the "thou shalt' and 'thou shalt not' commandments, not just the famous ten." Reb turned on her father. "Tell these folks how their theology of fear and conformity seduced you."

Frank faced his daughter. "You don't have a lot of tolerance, do you?" "Like father, like daughter," she said. Frank stood and said, "They employed a literalistic biblicism using proof-texting. Phil explained how that led to bibliolatry, worshiping the book, not the God in the book. They selected certain biblical passages that appeared to reduce complex moral dilemmas to simplistic solutions. That led to easy and certain moral conclusions, even for the most difficult moral quandaries. Basking in this self-righteousness produced a new addiction. I got high reducing moral issues to ten prohibitions." "Interesting," said Brad. "You got drunk on the commandments?"

Frank: "Yep. Look, alcohol can give you instant relief from pain, right? Complexities cause the pain of clear thinking, sound judgment, hard decisions, and personal responsibility, right? So you turn to alcohol for relief, right? Now, give up alcohol. The pain of complexity comes back, yes? Well, simplistic commandments dissolve complexity. A complex issue gets simplified to a black and white solution. Voila, no pain." Frank's face showed relief and regret.

"Dad, that was very abstract. May I tell them how your simplistic mind-set devastated me in a specific and personal case?" "Yes. Gently, please."

Reb looked at her father and began. "Mom became incurable, terminal. She was dying, but slowly, in a cold, sterile room with tubes stuck in everywhere and a breathing apparatus down her throat. She wanted to die at home as soon as she could. She said so to Nonnie and me. You wanted to keep her alive as long as you could. Partly because you just did, partly because of that commandment about 'Thou shalt not kill.'"

Frank held his hand before her face. "Enough. I need to say the rest." His face, drawn and pale, looked out the window. He walked up close to it and spoke in a voice slow and quiet. "I knew she wanted to die and to die on the island. I also knew that the voice of God had told Moses to tell the Israelites not to kill. The pastor in that church in Manchester had threatened me with condemnation to hell for disobeying God's law." He turned to the room. "I was as addicted to that mind-set as I ever was to vodka. Two different kinds of chains, same result." Back to the window. "Not proud of that. Very sorry I did that." Emily moved to him, put an arm around his waist. "Very proud of you for facing it with us," she said. Phil and Brad joined them. Reb stayed put. So did Hal.

12 Further Questings Through Biblical Parallels

The days between the gatherings had further discussions and explanations and unraveling of the emotional tangles so that when the group got back together, Phil could say, without prologue, "Moving along. When the Israelites came out of Egypt, shed their bondage, and made their covenant with God, they remained self-centered. As they began their long pilgrimage through the wilderness toward Canaan, they behaved like children let out of school, wanting everything and appreciating nothing." He wrote on the easel, "(7) Wandering in the wilderness."

"That's me," said Frank. "All this stuff is mixed together. All that time I manipulated that land-grab, built that gross house, segregated my family from one another in pleasure suites, drank, unfairly profited, lived for material wealth, power, and possessions, worshiped the Bible, relied on commandmentism, centered on self-righteousness. All wandering in the wilderness." Frank looked exhausted. Emily brought him ice water. "Water?," said Frank, "how about vodka?" A little laughter lightened things up while Frank emptied the glass. He pointed to it and said, "A pale substitute for my old friend who turned out to be a serpent."

Phil said, "Everybody still willing to press on into Canaan?" Consent. "That was the Israelites' last stop. They occupied the so-called Promised Land and discovered that the locals had great harvests because they worshiped little fertility idols called Baals. Or so the Canaanites said. The Israelites began worshiping these little idols also." Frank wrote "(8) Idolatry" on the easel. "The Israelites justified this with Why not? Gotta eat. They knew, of course, that worshiping idols violated the Sinai covenant, but, hey, c'mon, be reasonable.

"Now the Bible states over and over that the Sinai covenant had an irreducible center: fidelity. God promised everlasting love, abiding fidelity to the well-being of Israel. God expected commensurate love for God and steadfast fidelity to God and to God alone. Idol worship violated that covenant. Worshiping any value higher than God disrespected the covenant. The Israelites did worship the Baals, over and over again. Sometimes they worshiped in overt religious rituals. Sometimes they worshiped by the way they ran their lives and set their values. Does that have any counterpart in your life, Frank?"

"Of course it does, Phil. Isn't this getting tedious? All the stuff I've recounted had its roots in idolatry. I worshiped money, power, status. I worshiped alcohol. I worshiped my boats and cars. They all promised easy pleasure, satisfaction, indulgence but no sacrifice."

He looked out the window. "And I still have no replacement for them. I don't believe in God, so I can't center my life there. I don't find nature worthy of worship, as Nonnie does. I have no service to perform, no contribution to other people. So even though I've given up my idols, I still have an empty life, pointless, sailing in circles, reading, talking, sleeping. My wife died a recluse in our own house, my daughter left home as soon as she could and still thinks I'm a jerk. I ended up alone in my castle of riches, a pathetic zero. Now I have no castle, no riches, just the zero."

Hal, Reb, Nonnie, and Phil moved in around Frank. "No sniveling, buddy," said Nonnie. "You'll clean up good," said Reb. Hal put his hand on his son's shoulder.

* * * * *

Nonnie stood and got in front of the group. "Phil, I want to talk. I don't say much here because I don't buy the Christian template for spirituality. Never have, never will. But sometimes you do touch some of my cherished notions, sometimes, such as this idolatry.

"In my years in jail . . . ." She had to stop, since they all made such a noisy reaction to these words. "You didn't know about old Nonnie's felonious youth? Didn't know I did hard time for snatching a baby out of a baby carriage in front of the Old Ebbitt Grill when wee babe's mommy and daddy weren't looking? There's a parable for you to ponder. I got caught a few blocks away. That was in 1914, I a bare teenager. Speaking of street urchins, I had been one for some time. So they put me away for years and years till I walked out during the Pearl Harbor confusion in 1941, just like Mr. Toad as a washerwoman. Changed my identity, took up residence down on Nomanisan with Nick Spooner, and had Lilly-Belle soon after.

"Anyhow, as I was saying, my jail years gave me nothing but time to read. I read everything, educated myself. I defined a centering principle: no dependencies. Since I built Meshach in 1942 and had Lilly-Belle, I have lived close to the land and the water. I grow my own food, make my own way, and take time for talking and reading. So I have declared independence from material clutter. I have watched you people fritter away your time and money acquiring, protecting, repairing, replacing, and in short, worshiping all your things.

"Worship? I know, you don't pray to your dishwasher. But devoting major time and resource to something and depending upon it shows me that it has major worth to you. As in worth-ship, or wor-ship. So, yes, you do worship your dishwashers and the like.

"I know the biblical narrative. Phil gets it right. Israel got seduced into worshiping the little Canaanite Baals that promised to make them happy the easy way with guaranteed fertility and protection from the bad guys. What a laugh. The easy way never works. Baals don't work. Idols don't work. Anything you want you got to labor for.

"Now here you people are, struggling to find meaning beyond your comfortable lives. A spirituality beyond your stuff. Well, I say congratulations. Most rich folks just lounge around on their comforts and buy their release from labor and pain on the open market. Look at Frank. The Baals snared him for twenty years and it took his conniving daughter to lay a challenge on his latent spirit and jolt his sorry self into reality. Now he's showing promise, and you people are helping him help you. Sounds like interdependence to me, the best kind."

She sat down. Emily rang the bell. This break time had some lively talk, people trying to get more detail out of Nonnie about her adventures. And they found out how she could accept no dependencies at the same time she lived by her motto, "no man is an island."

* * * * *

Reb said, "In my comparative literature class we had to write a short paper on a piece of world literature. Wanna hear mine? 'The plot of the Old Testament starts with God creating equilibrium, humankind causing disequilibrium, God acting with grace to call Abraham, empathizing with Israel's bondage, making a covenant of unconditional love, and staying with Israel in the wilderness.

"But we see the most striking feature in those Old Testament books which tell about the kingdoms of Israel and Judah. For six centuries the Israelites would worship God for a while, then would slip into worshiping Baals. The prophets called them over and over to fidelity to God and God alone. But why should they do that when specialized idols promised easy and immediate solutions to problems? And God, in contrast, promised only fidelity to Israel, to be always present in times of trouble.

"Israel had to choose between worshiping the one massive presence of God or the many utilitarian Baals. Very hard, in the middle of a drought and infertility and enemies approaching to steal your land and family to keep your allegiance to God and God alone. In reading those books you see this tendency over and over. They failed to remain faithful to God. Obvious.

"What's not so obvious is God's amazing response to their infidelity. You have to watch for it. You'll see that God nonetheless remained faithful to them, inviting them over and over to return to communion. Israel could depend upon only one constant: God's grace, God's steadfast love, God's refusal to abandon them no matter how often they abandoned God. Amazing.'"

Polite applause. Phil wrote on the easel, "(9) Nonetheless, grace-love."

Frank said, "I have struggled to see any similarity between that account of grace and my life. I can see this much: that Nonnie stayed with me while I played the jackass, so did Lilly-Belle, so did Emily and Brad. I guess that's grace."

Frank turned toward his father. Hal's face showed ambivalence. Frank said, "Now, Father. You and I have talked long about how I believed you abandoned me and how you believed I had betrayed you. We agreed that we both got it wrong. So when I leave you out of that list of people who stayed with me, I mean no disrespect."

Hal: "Understood. Hard for me to say this. We both suffered horrible trauma when my sweet Sibyl died. I crumbled, lost my bearings. I did and said things I regret. And now I'm grateful for our reunion. Doesn't change the past, changes only our relationship now. Moving on." Phil: "A display of grace from you both. Thanks for letting us be with you in that."

Emily spoke up. "Discovering that fact of the biblical narrative changes my concept of God forever. The idea of grace has had no value for me, just an abstract doctrine. Here God enacted grace right in plain sight. It defined the meaning of the Old Testament for me. It converted my concept of a wrathful God to a God of grace and steadfast love. Thanks."

Brad said, "I found that interesting, but not persuasive. Big problem for me: If God forgives everything, where's the enforcement? What's to prevent me from wholesale promiscuity if there's no penalty? People need accountability."

"I agree," said Hal, "sort of. I'm thinking, however, that grace inspires grace, that people who experience forgiveness and reconciliation are not likely to exploit grace." A lively exchange followed, including an exploration of Dietrich Bonhoeffer's ideas on cheap grace and costly grace.

* * * * *

At the next gathering, Phil said that he had asked Brad and Emily to summarize what they had heard Frank say about his life in parallel to the biblical plot.

Brad read, "To review: Frank grew up in a peaceful, stable family. A terrible accident and his reaction to it upset this equilibrium and led to his alienation from his family and positive prospects. Nonnie called him to remedy the damage he had caused. His actions led to his bondage. Frank recovered from his coronary and shook loose from alcohol; that is, he made an exodus into a new kind of life. But he fell under the spell of a church which offered him an easy certainty, a code of legalisms. It launched him on his journey through a spiritual wilderness that led to a land of plenty with many false gods. He worshiped these for their seductive offerings, thus separating himself from his family and friends. Nonetheless, his friends stayed with him, a tacit invitation to return to the communion of friendship." Reb said, "Bravo, Brad!"

Brad said, "Thank Emily. She wrote it. Remember, please, my sacred atheism." Reb: "Bravo, Emily!" Phil: "So we see that the Bible gives a mythic account of a cycle that repeats in ordinary lives: First, God provides equilibrium. Second, we cause disequilibrium: alienation. Third, nonetheless. Here comes the "nonetheless" dynamic, the most arresting feature of the whole biblical narrative. Nonetheless, God neither condemns nor abandons humankind as you would reasonably expect. The Old Testament, we have seen, documents this cycle in the history of Israel."

Hal said, "I got a problem. I used to read those children's books with titles like 'the story of the Bible.' They had no plot. Just random narratives." "Yes," said Phil. "Those books and adult books as well don't seem to notice the larger beginning-to-end narrative. But it's there."

Hal said, "Fair enough, if you say so. I may have to read the thing myself to validate this provocative notion." "Please do." "But I've got another problem. This term grace-love that you seem to like. I think I get it about God and Israel. But what about, let's say, me and Frank?"

Phil said, "Yes. Suppose I say something to you, something deeply alienating that deserves breaking our friendship. And you do break our friendship, drop me. We split. In our culture, that would be an expected consequence of my alienating behavior. But suppose you do just the opposite. Suppose you forgive me and restore our relationship as an unconditional gift of reconciliation. That we would call grace, a gracious act. Does that help?"

"Well, in the abstract it helps. Hard to imagine actually doing it." Phil noticed Frank's body stiffening. And Hal looking out the window. Phil said, "Of course. In our culture we don't do it right out in the open. We don't often say, 'I am angry, but I love you anyhow. I'm sorry. Let's start fresh.' But whether overt or tacit, any willingness to make a new, revised relationship deserves a strong term like grace-love. It's an awkward term. The Hebrews had a single word, *hesed*, and so did the Greeks, *agape*.

"I think that these 'nonetheless' words point to a central meaning of the Bible: God operates in generous grace-love. God has gracious and loving policies. The Bible as a whole does not show a wrathful God. We do not see God building a case against you, threatening to damn you for your failures, judging your acceptability. To the contrary, the Bible shows us God always inviting return to communion with God and one another, always creating a new and improved you. And you can always accept that invitation."

"Well," said Emily, "up until the time you die. Then you go up or down, up if you've been good, down if not." Hal went rigid. Reb shook her head: "No." Phil said, "So some churches say. We'll get to that big question later." "As you have been saying for some long time now, Phil," said Hal.

Phil smiled. "I think we could all benefit now from reading Jonathan Bryan's book called *Nonetheless, God Retrieves Us: What a Yellow Lab Taught Me about Retrieval Spirituality.*" Nonnie said, "Who's he?"

13 The Christ Event

After a caffeine break, Phil leaned on the mantle. "Moving right along now. After all that idolatry over all those centuries that rejects all that grace, you wouldn't think God would offer further grace. But God has the ultimate act of grace yet to give. The gift came in an ordinary Galilean peasant. Named Jesus. We have three things to do about Jesus. Clarify what we mean in saying that Jesus incarnates God. Get a grip on the concept of his crucifixion. And work out some meanings of his resurrection. Three things, which taken together we can call the Christ event. Incarnation, Crucifixion. Resurrection.

"So, first, incarnation. Hang on for another dose of cosmic work. The ancient Greeks had a concept of the *logos*, the order and architecture of the universe, the unifying principles, how it all works. If we ask John the evangelist and Paul the apostle how we got here, they answer, 'God's *logos* gives the universe its order; the *logos* creates all.'

"Next we ask a scientific theist what happens and the answer comes back 'transcendent God originated the Big Bang, which is using natural laws to create all that is.'

"Notice that the two answers converge in concepts so similar we can say that the Big Bang is the scientific equivalent of the biblical *logos*."

"You mean," said Nonnie, "that once again we can condense your verbiage, wordy Phil, into a bumper sticker? 'Logos and Big Bang, Incarnated, Cosmic Architects and General Contractors.'"

"No, Nonnie, I don't mean that. This is not plural. If you want a bumper sticker, try 'Big Bang Logos, Incarnated, Cosmic Architect-Contractor.'"

Emily stood. "Enough," she said, "Get milk and cookies."

* * * * *

During the break Phil opened his Bible to show the exact passages from John and Paul:

"In the beginning when God created the heavens and the earth, the earth was a formless void and darkness covered the face of the deep, while a wind from God swept over the face of the waters. Then God said, "Let there be light"; and there was light. And God saw that the light was good; and God separated the light from the darkness." (Genesis 1.1-4)

"In the beginning was the Word [*logos*], and the Word was with God, and the Word was God. He was in the beginning with God. All things came into being through him, and without him not one thing came into being. . . . And the Word became flesh [Jesus] and lived among us." (John 1.1-3, 14)

"He [Jesus] is the image of the invisible God, the firstborn of all creation; for in him all things in heaven and on earth were created, things visible and invisible . . . . All things have been created through him and for him." (Colossians 1.15-16)

* * * * *

In a few minutes Phil said, "Hold that cosmic thought and let's do Jesus, alive and well, fully human. Now bring back the thought about the incarnation of the *logos*. Jesus, son of Mary, incarnates the transcendent *logos*. So we see that Jesus has two attributes: fully human, fully God incarnate.

"But there's more. The New Testament says that Jesus was born, grew up in Galilee, was baptized, called disciples, taught and healed. We see that he is approachable, communicative, strengthening, motivating, energizing, reconciling, healing, making whole. Now remember, this is fully human, fully God doing these things. So while Jesus incarnates transcendent God, Jesus also represents God right here, right now, present among us. The word for that is immanent. Combine all that and we see transcendent God, immanent.

"And how did Jesus of Nazareth spend his time among us? As the *logos* incarnate, doing what the *logos* does: creating. Creating wholeness out of brokenness and illness. Creating community out of division. Creating hope out of despair. Creating communion with God out of alienation from God. Creating liberty from the guilt of failure to conform to every demand of the law. Creating inclusion of the outcasts within the closed circle of self-righteous pietists.

"Jesus dramatized life centered on God. He taught a new way to live in relationships of reconciliation, not alienation and anger. He encouraged communities of love and grace, not self-centered individualism. He showed utter dependence upon God and God alone, not the Baals of artificial salvation. He showed internal serenity despite conditions of anxiety and distrust. He showed kindness, empathy, and compassion to counter society's indifference to human needs. His life demonstrated how God-centered *shalom* displaces disequilibrium and disharmony. He gave confidence that God yearns to heal brokenness. And he said plainly that God does not, not punish sin by inflicting illness and poverty."

Reb said, "Please. What's this word *shalom?*" "Hebrew word for equilibrium, harmony, peace, everything working together. Scientists show us how every action has an equal and opposite reaction. That's a symptom of *shalom*, of how all in creation balances, compensates, corresponds. Think ecology, the balance of nature. The underlying order and reliability of the universe shows its *shalom*. If I say to you, '*shalom*,' Reb, I wish you all the serenity that comes from a life in balance and equilibrium, equanimity. The absence of alienation, imbalance." "Oh," said Reb. "Believe it or not," said Nonnie, "the word 'whole' derives from the ancient root of *shalom*. Wishing you *shalom* wishes you wholeness, fulfillment, completeness." "Oh," said Reb. "*Shalom*."

Phil said, "Back now to Jesus' time. People in Judaism had

come to believe that God demanded that everyone conform to unyielding legalisms, enforcing these with vindictive, punitive judgments. Repudiating this false image, Jesus showed people that God offers steadfast love, forgiveness, and grace. Or to put it another way, Jesus carried out the same policies of grace-love, *hesed* and *agape,* that God used with Israel from the beginning."

Reb said, "You mentioned that Jesus was dramatizing life centered on God? Meaning that he was enacting God's character?" "It's an interesting idea," said Emily, "that Jesus would not talk much about God's attributes but would create, in person, concepts of how God is, how God relates to us, God's policies." The group fell silent, considering. Brad studied the ceiling. "Farfetched. But for the sake of exploring it, I'd offer a tentative thought: that your cosmic Christ, your so-called *logos,* your presumed original agent of creation might . . . might, unlikely but just might . . . be still, now, creating." Phil said, "Creating what, Brad?" "Hell, Phil, how would I know? This is your territory." "Yeah," said Phil.

"Oh go ahead and say it, Brad." Nonnie headed for the coffee pot. "You guys like toying with fancy categories. Brad, you're intrigued, maybe hooked. This stuff feeds your intellect, but your pride gags on religion. Repeat after me: The *logos* initiated the original creation, continued creating new ways of understanding God, and is still creating new concepts. There. Was that so hard? I don't buy it, since its presupposition is bunk, but I get it." "What presupposition?" "God. Not."

Phil stood up. "Anyhow, we've taken a look at the incarnation. Moving on to the crucifixion of Jesus. Not everyone welcomed Jesus' ideas and actions. The religious authorities feared Jesus' image of God forgiving and reconciling. They needed to use punitive legalisms to keep the masses fearful and submissive. His teachings exposed the hypocrisy of their liberties, power, and self-indulgence. So when Jesus went to Jerusalem for a Passover, they colluded with the Romans to try him on trumped-up charges of blasphemy. They condemned him to death by crucifixion.

"Jesus saw this coming. He could have left town before he faced the charges. But he let them take him. In that sense he sacrificed himself, showing us how far he would go for our well-being. That's love. Of course he wanted to avoid the pain. Nonetheless, he did the sacrifice. He gave his life in love for us. He demonstrated God's boundless love for all humankind, God's boundless yearning for reconciliation with humankind, God's boundless grace."

Brad said, "You say 'us.' You mean love for those people who follow him?" "No, I mean for everyone. All humankind. All? Everyone. And that means you, Brad." Brad made a face. "No, not me."

Phil said, "At least, we can see all this in hindsight. It's not what those folks saw on that gruesome Friday. They saw that God had finally gotten fed up, had given up on humanity, had finally said, 'Killing Jesus are you? Well, I give up. That's the worst. Forget it. I'm finished with you.'

"Because look: cruel, evil, malicious people hammered spikes through his wrists and ankles to a cross stuck into a sun-beaten hilltop. That good, loving Jesus with his sound teaching and generous nature and gift of healing and great promises of hope was hanging in agony from nails through his wrists into that cross.

"Since Jesus was entirely human, his mind and body were suffering as much as ours would. He knew that Judas had betrayed him, Peter had denied him, and his disciples had abandoned him. He suffered fear, hopelessness, and loss, all signifying humiliating defeat. All the forces of death and destruction, all the hatred, all the negatives, all the denials, all the suspicion in this broken world were brought to bear on this man."

"But wait," said Hal, "if he was God, he knew how this was coming out. Short pain, long glory." "I don't think so," said Phil, "remember, fully human. He suffered as much as you and I would. Same nerve endings as ours, same emotional reactions. Jesus died in excruciating pain.

"He hung from that cross, broken, for some six hours while his body weight constricted his lungs and breathing. He suffered pain, thirst, shock. He could no longer get enough oxygen to his brain. He finally died from the lingering pain of spikes and suffocation and defeat. His heart and brain died. He died dead. Destroyed and unrecoverable. Totally finished. Ruined. Gone.

"You can't get any more dead than Jesus was dead. From mid-afternoon his body hung lifeless from the cross until sunset, when disciples took him down. By then, in that sun, his flesh would have begun to decompose. Women wrapped his broken body head to foot. Friends buried him in a tomb.

"So, what to remember about the crucifixion? The result of fear and hatred; unjust, fraudulent; voluntary, signifying sacrificial love; extreme physical and emotional suffering; absolute, final death, return to nothingness.

"We've now examined two-thirds of the Christ event: the incarnation and the crucifixion. On to the resurrection.

"Jesus' corpse went into the tomb on Friday evening. On Sunday, at first light, women discovered not only that the tomb was empty but that Jesus was greeting them. As the days went on, he appeared to various people. The Bible says that he was clothed, not enshrouded, that his wounds were visible and touchable, and that disciples recognized him as he walked, talked, and ate with them.

"What's this? As you can understand, this apparent 'coming back to life' caused extreme confusion, dispute, joy, astonishment. And various explanations.

"Seven main explanations have survived the centuries. Choose one:

"One. Resuscitation. On Friday Jesus never actually died, but went into suspended animation or a coma. God resuscitated him in the tomb and he emerged. He came back to the same mortal life that he had before, warmed over. But rather than die again and stay dead, he ascended as a human body into heaven.

"Two. Apparition. God came to earth disguised as Jesus. So everybody experienced only an apparition of a human body, which was never really human. His seeming death was like a video display, nothing but excellent visual effects. Same for his resurrection appearances. Fade to zero and call it ascension.

"Three. Hallucination. Jesus had fully human life and death. And he impressed the disciples so much that they were ready to believe that God had brought him back from the dead. And so, in their spiritually overheated and deluded imaginations, they hallucinated him. His resurrection condition lived only as a figment.

"Four. Metaphor. The story has little or no historical validity, but it does serve as a strong metaphor to illuminate God's power to bring new life out of whatever has become old and dead.

"Five. Fabrication. The whole narrative emerged from desperate disciples who fabricated the story and lied to prospective converts.

"Before we proceed to our last two explanations, let's deal with a question. Could any of those first five explanations transform people's lives? Transform people enough for them to become vulnerable to persecution, to reorganize their lifestyles, to dedicate their living to the risen Christ? Probably not. But verifiable history has documented that untold millions of people have indeed adopted a conviction that God became physically incarnate in a fully human, fully divine Jesus alive, crucified, and resurrected Christ in whom all was made new. Here we confront a reality: in the Christ event God did change the direction of history, change the world. That could happen only if Jesus, fully human and fully divine, died bodily dead and then appeared bodily resurrected to many disciples.

"Personally, I had to work my way through those first five hoping for an easy out. When they failed, I adopted the next:

"Six. Standard Resurrection. Jesus died, dead. On the third day he appeared in a visible, physically functioning form. Not resuscitated human, not apparition, not hallucination. But yes, a unique category called a resurrection body, the risen Christ. This had two distinctive characteristics: it was simultaneously physical and non-physical. Physical, in that his disciples could touch him, walk, talk and eat with him. Non-physical, in that his body was able to pass through closed doors, become visible and then invisible. So, God resurrected Jesus' corpse into a transformed reality, a new order of life, a new creation unlike anything ever before or since.

"This standard resurrection has served well as mainstream, Easter Sunday stock in trade. But over time it lost my commitment.

It offered nothing more than a comforting assurance that all would be well after my death if I behaved myself. I suspected the resurrection means more than this personal benefit. So I developed my Resurrection Upgrade. It's a work in progress. Here it is:

"The resurrection gives the biblical message its ultimate meaning. How? First, God creates us in communion. Then we commit continual acts of alienation. Nonetheless, God continually invites us back. Then the Christ event, the climax of the Bible. God becomes incarnate in Jesus, suffers self-sacrificial crucifixion, and dies. That ends the old creation. Finished. Completed. As Jesus said from the cross, 'tetelestai,' 'it is finished, accomplished, fulfilled.'

"Now, against that background I can say with complete confidence that God resurrected Jesus' corpse into a transformed reality, a new order of life, a new creation unlike anything ever before or since. And I can say with complete confidence that the resurrection inaugurates this new creation. Like the original Big Bang, all is being created anew. And in our new resurrectional condition, we serve as the Body of Christ. We work to reconcile all humankind into fulfilled communion. Now, Frank?"

14 Parallels with the Christ Event

Frank got a cup of coffee. Others topped up too. "Phil, I cannot and will not attempt to fit my experience into that account of the Christ event. You'll have to settle for a plain vanilla version. So, I have worked out that I too had an incarnational segment in my life.

"You said something a month ago that kept me awake. You wondered what spark ignited the fire that burned off my self-absorption, my self-serving habits. You said you suspected it happened when Lilly-Belle died. She left me alone, with only a daughter who hated me. This realization unlocked my potential.

"You said this thing: The original creation that God initiated continues. The Big Bang continues to bang. The causes that originated then are still causing things to happen, from causes to effects. God continues to create brand new realities. Realities tangible and intangible.

"Then you got mystical, telling me that God's creative power carries a spirit of love. You said it's a universal constant. You said that God's love for us creates love in us. Like so many of your unassailable generalities, your cerebral constructs, I can't dispute it.

"But you did get off a zinger that caught my attention. You said that when Lilly-Belle died and my daughter certified her hatred for me, God created love in my heart, a little spark of love. You said that love came to birth in that crisis, that it grew like the Grinch's heart.

"From being just mystical you got just weird. You said that

the little infant love in my heart resembled the little infant Jesus. Both incarnated God's love. Phil, do you know how offensive that sounded to me? I nearly abandoned you at that point. Nothing about me can resemble anything about Jesus. Stop it. Don't lay that on me.

"Trouble was, once I settled down, I realized that something like love for Reb did start on my bed of self-inflicted pain. I realized I did have this empty life, a profound nothingness, as nothing as the nothing which the Big Bang began to fill and fulfill.

"I remember that I looked over my life and assigned numbers to events in a sort of mental balance sheet. The events in the liabilities column didn't balance the events in the assets columns. I don't like losses of any kind, in business or in life.

"That's when I first noticed a tiny sense of yearning, as tiny as an embryo. I felt an emerging need for more relationship with others. I remember feeling that something wasn't okay about what Reb had become and not become for me."

Frank looked into the fireplace. "I suppose, as strange as it is to say this, that a tiny yearning could be an incarnational moment, when the love of God came alive in my parched life.

"Phil, you and I discussed this little spark of yearning to love, and to be loved. We decided that it did ignite love for Reb I had never even felt, let alone expressed. In that crisis about the memorandums and log books, it burst into a flame that burned off some selfish dross and left the beginning of concern for her well-being."

Frank had been walking around the room during this soliloquy, ending behind Nonnie's chair. "I debated what to do about Reb, whether to crucify her little sneaky self or show her this new love. Trouble was, I had always confused loving with liking, and I did not like this daughter. I was, it's true, beginning to feel a deep concern for her well-being. Turns out that was the love. Liking her would have to wait. Still waiting, but it's coming." His daughter smiled a little smile, very little. He returned it with a broad smile.

Phil began with "Okay, we've explored what the incarnation of God, known to us as Jesus, demonstrated for us in his life. And we've seen how Frank experienced an incarnational growth of the love that God has for us.

"Frank, Reb, Hal, Nonnie, and I discussed next how Frank had a crucifixional experience. To understand it, we had to define a category called 'crucifixional events,' when some valued feature of your life is lost and gone forever, finished, terminated. Destroyed and unrecoverable. Not just injured, comatose, or missing. Totally finished. Like Jesus, ruined. Dead. Gone. You're left with nothing but memory and wreckage. Your loss causes emotional and/or physical pain.

"We came up with examples. Good health is permanently compromised. A strong business fails. Love turns bitter. The pink slip appears. Your best work still fails to yield the college degree. Your life-savings are lost. A dream evaporates. A trust is betrayed. Natural calamity wrecks a lovely work. Life's work slides into insignificance. A family shuns the disgraced brother.

"We made another category: the self-sacrificial crucifixional event. You deliberately sacrifice something valuable in order to benefit another person. You sacrifice a personal advantage for another's well-being. You compromise your personal desire in order to provide a middle ground that's better for all. You want retribution but instead you give a gift of grace. The staff chips in big shares of their savings to pay a co-worker's life-saving surgery. You set aside your pride to make a painful apology.

"So crucifixional events come in two forms: destruction by an outside force and destruction by self-sacrifice to benefit another. What have you got for us here, Frank?"

Frank said, "The conversations about this nearly broke me. First, it was hard enough to contemplate for the first time the grossness of Jesus' crucifixion. Brutal. Then, looking through the lens of Jesus' crucifixion at my own suffering did put things into perspective. Sure, in the sense of 'crucifixional,' as we defined it, what I went through had a certain pale resemblance to Jesus' ordeal. But only in a stretched abstraction."

"Okay, Frank," said Nonnie, "so it wasn't such a big deal, relative to Jesus. How about what you admitted about crucifying your daughter?"

"Oh, thanks, Nonnie. Good to have a reminder of what I was trying to forget. Yes, it can't be concealed. In this sense I crucified Reb on a cross of materialism. I gave her everything from the store and nothing from the heart."

"Think nothing of it, pops," said Reb, "I thought that chartreuse Kharmann-Ghia had a lot of heart, as soon as I repainted it."

Frank gave her an ambiguous glance and topped up his coffee. She stood and said she had some stuff to lay out in the crucifixional department. And she spent several minutes struggling to articulate that she had tried to crucify him on a cross of subterfuge and false accusation. She explained how she had forged documents to incriminate him enough to force him out of his firm. And how she had made the whole thing so transparent he had to know she did it. How she wanted to watch him struggle between accusing his own daughter and losing his position.

She went on to disclose that she had never even thought of the third option she had left open by mistake. She said, "So Dad, why didn't you just get an expert to certify that the handwriting belonged to some unknown someone? And the ink was not old enough? You could have had it both ways: I'm not implicated, and neither are you."

"Good question, darling daughter. But how then would you have known that I love you? I had to let you see me sacrifice Grant International, my most treasured asset, to protect you. In that third option you wondered about, I would have lost you. Anyhow, why would I want to go back to that lonely, empty life? Why would I want to lose you and keep Reprise, of all the ugly houses? I had grown past all that." Reb looked sideways at her father. "Love me? What are you smoking?"

"So much for crucifixion," said Phil. "Next up, resurrection. Ever notice how good things sometimes emerge from bad? Jesus' crucifixion left nothing but a bloody corpse, but from that emerged something unique, the risen Christ. Just so a crucifixional event leaves nothing but the corpse of something wonderful from which emerges a resurrectional event. This happens enough that you could say, if a crucifixional event comes, can a resurrectional be far behind?

"Such as, failure in a business venture leads to a new vocation. Into dark hopelessness a new illumination of possibilities. Illness is not cured, but is healed. The loss of one structure clears the way for a new and better structure. Bitter defeat engenders re-doubled determination. A wrecked friendship re-structured on an all-new basis. We turn our alienation into reconciliation on a new basis.

"So, Frank, any resurrectional event for you?"

"Yeah, and am I glad to get out of all that depressing account of my life and into this. After Lilly-Belle died, you recall, Reb lay that trap for me. It caught me between two wretched choices. Either choice would, in this metaphorical sense, 'crucify' me. And then that strange wrinkle, the little spark of love for my daughter emerging to lead me to choose self-sacrifice.

"And having made that choice, I walked out of Grant International into emptiness, no identity, no work, no income, no life as I had known it. Nothing, or, as you like to say, Phil, *nihil*. The old Frank became a corpse. Dead. Kaput.

"Then began this long resurrectional process. It may have looked like fun, liquidating possessions, traveling. But I wandered lonely as a cloud. Lost identity. Wife gone, daughter gone, position gone. Belongings and house and cars and boats, all gone. Nothing left but a boat and an annuity. Never had any spiritual life, so I couldn't lose that. But I know now that I was living an empty existence, a vacuum of meaning.

"That sail down the river got me to the cross on St. Clement's Island. I still don't know what to make of that. It moved me. Don't know how or why.

"Living in Misty Cove has given me new friendships. I've accrued spiritual assets. Nonnie rallied around. We ate fish together, told lies about the old days, told hard truth. Phil and Nonnie pulled all sorts of shenanigans to get me and Reb and Hal together. We knew what you were doing and, you must admit, we put up little resistance. All part of my resurrectional process. These conversations have illuminated how it all fits together. Given meaning to a life that looked pointless.

"I have found, then, that the loss Reb caused, the nothingness it left, became a seedbed for new life. Phil, you'd probably say something pedantic like 'a new creation, *ex nihilo.*'

"You're quite right," said Phil, "because I think you had a spiritual Big Bang in your deathly tomb of nothingness. It enlivened that spark of love and started the new creation of the new, new Frank."

15 New Identities in the Body of Christ

Phil said, "Now, the disciples experienced the reality of Jesus' resurrection body. They ate, walked, talked with him. But the bodily Christ soon disappeared. Ascended, they said. This left everyone confused and leaderless.

"But they also discovered that this experience was transforming their lives. They began to realize two astounding things: One, that in the resurrection God had made all creation new and that they were now living in this new creation. Two, that now that Jesus was gone they themselves had become the continuing body of the risen Christ.

"These realizations led them to a new sense of purpose. But what? Some said, So we'll get into heaven. Others said, To drive the Romans away. Yet others, To make everyone Christians. And others, To be forgiven our sins.

"But some of these transformed people said, To complete what God in Christ started here among us. They debated what exactly that was. After much experience, much trial and error, they decided on their mission: Be the Body of Christ. Be the arms and legs and voices and ears and feet of continuing Jesus. Do what Jesus had done: teach and heal and bring others into the body. Give, serve, show forth the love and grace of God. Reconcile, close the gaps estranging one from another. Become a unified people of God. Become, indeed, the new incarnation of God in this mortal life, the Body of Christ. And ultimately reconcile the ancient alienations, bring all humankind into communion with God and one another. That would be the bottom line.

"They went to work telling others about Jesus and the Christ event. The story transformed untold numbers of people all around the Mediterranean. These new Christians combined into communities called *ekklesia*, meaning churches. They were the mangers for the infant Body of Christ. They tried to be in communion with God and one another."

Emily came to her feet. She said, "Phil as you know, I got a pretty good dose of Bible in my childhood. What you just said disagrees with what I heard, and heard clearly: God created Adam and Eve, who sinned against God, so God expelled them from Eden and condemned all their descendants to hell. Thus they sinned the more. God, exceedingly angry, sent Jesus to be a scapegoat and die for our sins. They crucified him and that made God feel much better, now that the debt was paid off. But Jesus came back from the dead and, ever since, Easter has been a great celebration, everyone in finery. The apostles went out to try to save souls from God's wrath, to help them be moral and try their best to get into heaven past Saint Peter, who is taking names and kicking people into hell. At the Judgment Day Jesus will show up again and judge who gets in and who doesn't. I ask you Phil, who's got this right? The pastors who said that, or you?"

"Phil said, "They said correctly what a lot of churches believe, Emily, more or less. If you choose Bible passages carefully, you can construct a theology like that. And it makes a difference. If a religious authority, a pastor says that the Bible says that God damns those who transgress, we live in fear and constant, futile striving to become worthy enough for God's acceptance.

"A variation on that theme declares that Christianity is all about morality, all about getting adherents to live moral lives. This focuses attention upon personal righteousness and leads to sanctimony.

"These ideas about our relationship with God cause further alienation from God, guilt, and self-absorption. Jesus spoke against such legalistic bondage to self-righteousness.

"By contrast, reading the Bible whole to discern a central message of grace-love does not select passages. Instead we examine the whole biblical narrative, trace its plot, and determine its meaning. I think that has more integrity than picking and choosing passages."

* * * * *

Nonnie stood up. "Phil, I wasn't listening to that stuff about the Bible because I want to challenge you on this Body of Christ. I have made quite clear that I come to these gatherings because you people amuse me and I like you. I am no Christian, so I am not in the Body of Christ. Presume no further." "Same for me," said Brad.

"Sorry, Nonnie, Brad. I apologize. Of course you may choose not to adopt a Christian identity. The Christian identity fits those who choose it. Not mandatory. No automatic penalty if you don't. No automatic reward if you do.

"But I have to say this. I think that in this new creation, God has indeed made every person a member of the Body of Christ. I don't think we have any more choice in this matter than we had any choice to become born in the first place and to be born human beings. Of course we are at liberty to choose what to do about this identity: accept it or reject it. Again, neither penalty nor reward either way.

"When I say that God made all things new in the resurrection, I mean that all people before, during and after Jesus are now the Body of Christ. That will enrage those who have reserved that status for the pious few, and I'm sorry for causing that rage, but I think what I think."

"Phil, that beats all I ever heard from you." Brad stood and stretched. "I followed it, but it is so abstract I don't think we can capture it without an air filter."

Emily said, "I like abstractions, but Phil, that one reminds me of the three kinds of sermons: solid, liquid, and gaseous. Guess which one. However, I do get it about communion in the Body of Christ. Here are my thoughts about this group. You guys have transformed me. Our work together has, it seems, transformed everyone here. We are not who we were when we started. We have new identities."

Reb said, "Me too. I see myself differently. It started when you, Grandma Nonnie, told me that narrative about how you decided in your youth to take on a new self-identity and then grow into it. So you decided that you descended from Huckleberry Finn on your father's side. That gave you a heritage of integrity and independence. And you decided that you descended from Hester Prynne and Pearl on your mother's side. That gave you a heritage of service as an outsider. You encouraged me to change my own self-identity into how I wanted to be. That planted a seed.

"The seed did not sprout till I realized that you, Dad, had committed an act of self-sacrifice for me. That gave me status I had never felt. It also made me feel very guilty, but I could not distinguish guilt from resentment, so I resented what I decided were your manipulative ways. I struggled with all this till a professor helped me see what I was doing to myself. Then the long process of reconciliation with my father. More self-sacrifice adding to a changing self-identity. From what you said about your resurrectional process, I think I may have gone through one too."

Phil said, "Self-identity? I wonder. Who am I, anyhow? What's the point of my life? I have struggled with these questions. Hear my story:

"Once upon a time, as a young adult, I went rock-climbing in the Blue Ridge. All by myself. Stupid. Somehow I must have slipped and fallen. A wonderful couple found me unconscious. Got me to a hospital. Stayed with me till I came back to consciousness. I had lost my memory. Didn't know who I was. No identification. No report of a missing person. I was no one. They helped me get going. I picked a name. Phil for my rescuers' love, as in the Greek *philos*, and Imbroglio because I seemed attracted to complex matters." Brad called out, "No! You, complex?" Phil ignored him while the room laughed. "I started at an amnesiac bottom, nobody, and built a new identity. I am now a lawyer and a minister.

"Over time I am discovering who I am way down deep, below the lawyer and the minister, who we all are, the identity we all share. We are members of the Body of Christ. We inhabit the new creation that came into being at Jesus' resurrection into the Christ of God."

Frank said, "So we have come to this, have we, disclosure of self-identity. Good, because my father and I have had a little chat, and we have a matter to bring up, one that you will, I trust, keep to yourselves."

Hal said, "Over the years since Sibyl died, I have tried to rebuild my identity. I have clung to one, a vocational identity: an engineer, builder of sturdy structures. Up until your return, Frank, I had almost abandoned my identity as a father. In only the time this group has been conversing I have looked for a spiritual answer like, like God's beloved, or something. Frank will now tell you how complicated this has become in the last few days."

Frank said, "In these last few days he and I have discussed something that happened when I was a teenager. I overheard my mother talking on the phone long distance to her mother in England. She said something I never understood, and I never asked. She said, 'No, Mum, I know what I know. Roland was killed in April of 1944. You couldn't remember seeing him in July of 1944. And please don't mention my fiancé again. He's dead. I have a husband and son.' Fiancé? I didn't know Mother had a fiancé before Father, someone named Roland.

"Then last year when I was doing all that traveling, I went to England, to Windermere, to see where Mother grew up, where she and Father courted and married, and where I was born. I passed an elderly couple sitting outside a pub. She had a face like Mother's. I noticed that they stared at me as I approached. Just as I went by, I heard the man say 'Roland!' I kept going and turned the first corner. Now I know why I'm so tall and slender and Mother and Father so short and stubby."

Hal said, "Perhaps some of you have had trouble understanding how Frank's lanky physique came from Sibyl's and my plump genes."

Frank said, "Further, the old couple in Windermere were also shorties and plump." Hal said, "So were my folks." "And yet further," said Frank, "when I was in Windermere, I found out that in 1944 you and Mother could not have gotten a marriage license in that short a time, let alone someone to marry you on a dock. My mother did some creative story-telling." He looked out the window toward the sky, the stars, the moon shining through the big oaks. "I think some tall, lanky Brit got Mother pregnant then went off to war and got killed, leaving an unwed mother." "Yep," said Hal, "not knowing what I was doing, I solved Sibyl's problem for her. After Frank grew up a bit, Sibyl decided I should know."

"Here's what impresses me," said Frank, "regardless of this irregularity, they loved each other with deep fidelity and affection. And they loved me, whoever sired me. They loved me. And my father loved me despite my blood lineage. He didn't have to do that. He could have rejected me. He didn't. In these last few days, as we have been edging toward reconciliation, I simply had to tell him what I had figured out. And why it moves me so deeply. As he and I have opened this up, we have grown close. We're back where we left off in early 1963, sailing Windermere that afternoon when Mother said, 'Life is short, art is long.'

"Now, with all this talk of self-identity, I am beginning to see that I am not who I thought I was. Not Hal's natural son, but his accepted son, someone he did not make but did take into his care. So I am accepting that I am accepted. Not only son of Prince Hal, my father, but also . . . ." Frank stopped. "Also this Christ's body? Too much. I can't go there. Scares me. More burden than I'm ready for."

* * * * *

Well, Frank, you and me. When I first encountered the implications of the concept of the Body of Christ (thirty-some years ago, around age forty), I recoiled. The concept threatened my comfortable status. I was going to church, more or less, for a thoughtful sermon, some prayers, decent coffee, and fine conversations with good friends. Then I found out this actual status: we are all the church. We don't go to church, we are church.

We are the risen Christ's resurrected body, continuing the work of incarnation. Sorry to get to preaching here, but I want you to know how serious I think this concept is and how little understood it seems to be. How did I get to forty without catching on? Dunno, but the realization laid an obligation on me I did not feel when I was just going to church.

16 Reconciliation

Phil said "We've established ways of thinking, through science, about universal origins, causality, evolution. That gave us a concept of God transcendent. And we have established ways of thinking about God immanent as found in the Bible.

"That led us to see that early on we, humankind, chose to alienate ourselves from God. But that God nonetheless chose to reconcile our alienation through the Christ event. Bringing us into the Body of Christ. Well, if Jesus went about reconciling, so do we, as the Body of Christ. How? We adopt Jesus' own reconcilational strategy. "Love God, love neighbor." This would replace the usual self-serving strategies of living to achieve self-righteousness.

"Paul's second letter to the church in Corinth expresses this. 'So if anyone is in Christ, there is a new creation: everything old has passed away; see, everything has become new. All this is from God, who reconciled us to himself through Christ, and has given us the ministry of reconciliation; that is, in Christ God was reconciling the world to himself, not counting their trespasses against them, and entrusting the message of reconciliation to us. So we are ambassadors for Christ, since God is making his appeal through us; we entreat you on behalf of Christ, be reconciled to God.'" (2 Cor 5.17-20)

* * * * *

Phil had breakfast with Frank. Frank was going on about how he was edging closer to a moment when he might be able to apologize to his daughter. "Doesn't seem right," he said, "that we can have these good conversations, the three of us, and yet remain unreconciled. She's living a few yards from me with Nonnie in My Coffin . . . ." He froze. He got a thousand-yard stare. He turned to Phil. "My God. What did I just say? Coffin? She might as well be dead. I want to bring her back into my life."

His friend asked whether he had any thoughts on how to make that happen. No, not a clue. Open to suggestions? Yes, anything. And so Phil explained how reconciliation works.

He noted that most conflict has two sides, that both of us have had some part in causing the conflict and the resulting alienation. What to do? He outlined the ideal process. As soon as the alienation is evident, you and I explain what went wrong and both acknowledge fault. We look for ways to avoid the problem in future. We apologize and forgive and carry on in a new equilibrium.

Being Phil, he could not resist pointing out that this pattern parallels the Christ event: initial equilibrium (incarnation) turns into alienation (crucifixion); however, through apology and forgiveness a new equilibrium emerges (resurrection).

Frank listened politely and asked Phil what about if one of us sees no harm done and won't work on reconciling. Phil explained that this calls for one-way reconciliation. You simply accept it as a reality and reconcile yourself to it. That would lead to your own new equilibrium, refusing to let it disrupt an otherwise good relationship.

"Okay," said Frank, "what's an apology?" "Well, if I feel remorse for something I have said or done, and I want to repair the damage that I have done to you, I can admit I've done wrong and ask for your forgiveness. Apologize." "Got it. Next, what is forgiveness?" Phil said, "If you decide, with sincere intent, to end your feelings of resentment or grievance or anger or desire to get even, or penalize, and move on, you could forgive me. You declare that the issue is closed, that the balance sheet shows zero, that the grudge is dead, that we have a new beginning, forgiven."

"Oh," said Frank, with the sort of wonderment we all had when the first Hubble pictures came out. "Is that when we say, 'forget it, it was nothing'"? "Sure," said Phil, "if it was nothing. Has your alienation from Reb been nothing? Think you will ever forget it?" Frank rolled his eyes. "Got it."

They talked over these things. Frank didn't know that on My Coffin Nonnie was presenting the same tutorial to Reb. As Phil got up to leave, he asked when Frank planned to do this thing. "Tomorrow," said Frank. Frank got a good night's sleep, interrupted by only an hour of night thoughts in which he rehearsed his plan.

* * * * *

The day dawned rainy. Nonnie watched Frank pull on a slicker and row over to My Coffin. She called to him, "What brings you out in this ducky weather?" "My daughter. It's time to heal these ancient wrongs. Will you help?" She almost said, What do think I've been doing?, but settled for "Sure." "Could you tell her how much I want to reconcile with her? Then she and I can talk together. And maybe you would sit with us while we talk." "I can do that." She had already primed Reb over the past few days to make this very approach to her father. This was better.

She helped father and daughter greet each other, sit together under the overhang, a gentle rain falling, and smile shyly at each other. But the embarrassment was thick enough to ladle, and self-consciousness paralyzed them. Neither could speak. Nonchalance said, apropos of nothing at all, "What does a five-hundred-pound canary say?" They looked at her blankly. "Here, kitty kitty." They had to laugh at the stupid thing. It may have been the first time father and daughter had ever laughed together.

Reb started. "You made me so angry when you . . . ." Nonchalance cut her off. "Sorry, Reb, but what really happened was that Frank did something and you made you angry. We talked about that. Only you can make you angry. Please continue."

Her granddaughter was unfazed. "I got so angry when you treated me like one of your employees: do the job or get sacked, behave myself or else, get a reward at the end of the year for satisfactory performance of duty, be a good daughter and stay in my suite, accept whatever gifts you gave and feel obligated to you for your beneficence, expect nothing out of me except compliance, no challenge, no encouragement, only fault-finding, agree with you when you protracted Mom's dying."

She looked a little breathless as she finished the inventory, but she looked pleased, too. Nonchalance had coached her well, and she had gotten off the entire salvo in one mighty heave.

Frank's jaw dropped a bit at the concentrated intensity of this outburst. He thought about some of its ambiguities, but let them pass. He had certainly gotten the drift of the whole message.

His coach had prepared him for a comparable message. He got going. "I reacted to your rebellious ways from way back. I felt your contempt for me, which perhaps I well deserved, but which also demoralized me yet further. All of this, though, I wrote off as you got older and I got wiser. But when you framed me, with evidence that could have wrecked me and my company, you made me . . . I mean . . . ." He smiled, Nonchalance smiled, Reb smiled. "I got very angry. I was enraged. And residue of that remains."

"I'm sorry, Daddy." "I'm sorry, Reb." "I forgive you, Daddy." "I forgive you, Reb."

* * * * *

Many days they spent getting to know each other. Long conversations. Long sails as Reb learned how to make Quest move through the wind and water at her will. As they resolved small emotional issues, trust grew, yielding mutual respect. Occasional setbacks depleted the gathering store for a spell, but later gains restored the trust and added to the deposit.

During the next session Reb was leaning on the dining room doorway munching cake. "I grew up with everything and nothing. When I learned the word *nihil* in Latin, I said, 'that's me and my life.' I had contempt for Dad, who neglected me, spoiled me, dissed me, bribed me, punished by deprivation, alienated his wife, my mother. I lived with that pious hypocrisy and mindless commandmentism so long I had no life values except survival through deceit. Then I discovered my mother's steadfast love, Nonnie's coaching, my professor's generous guidance, and the beautiful reconciliation with my father, who turns out to be a loveable jerk.

"The only concept of God I have ever had came from watching Dad tell me about God the commander, issuing commandments. Where is the love in that? Dad found a church that told him to be a father like the God they advertised: an autocratic God of behavior modification by threat." She ate more cake. The others gazed at her, amazed.

Her father walked to her side and hugged her. She tousled his hair. He said, "When my mother died I lost all sense of worthiness. I thought I had been the instrument of my mother's death, failing to notice the hairline crack each year, inviting her to go sailing. My father slammed me out of his life. My wife died and my daughter betrayed me.

"Standing here now speaking to you, with this woman at my side, demands my strongest willpower. It expresses my determination to be worthy. And I am in small steps gaining a sense of worthiness.

"I didn't want this child, but when she came regardless, I became obsessed with making a success of myself, to become worthy. I wanted to make a ton of money to salve guilt over Mother's death due to my carelessness, my invitation to go on that fatal sail.

"I have made and spent more money than all six of you. But at the height of my financial success, I collided with my daughter, discovered her contempt for me, realized that I had lost my wife and my daughter and my parents and had nothing to show for it but an immense bank account, a gauche house, and a firm that had helped pave over a beautiful peninsula. So I woke up. But to what dawn? Poverty, disgrace? Or a new way to live. To what purpose? What is the meaning of this new life? A sailboat cabin the size of my former broom closet? I have gotten a whiff of goodness in the world through my reconciliation with Reb. I hear Phil tell me that God is in the reconciliation business, that God came to earth to reconcile us. Oh? Not such a good track record so far, with all the conflict of every sort everywhere."

17 Communion

Hal spoke. "I have waited for a good time to tell you something. For some years now I have been going with Phil to St. Giles' Church. Never heard of it, have you. They're people who chose the name because St. Giles is the patron saint of lost causes. No one goes to this church except to try to recover from a lost cause, lost relationship, lost faith, lost job, lost hope. Don't have a church building. Lost interest in building one. So we meet in Everybody's Inn over on Route One on Sunday mornings before the place opens at noon. Don't have a minister. Lost the one we had. No real loss. Phil provides the communion service. So on behalf of our little congregation, I invite you to come for communion next Sunday."

This elicited a lively conversation, people trying to find out what communion is, why we would want to do it, and ending up in a ragged consensus to give it a try. "Nothing to lose," someone said. When the group broke up in the early evening, Frank walked out with Phil.

"Not sure I know what to do about this, Phil," said Frank. "I did church for a while some years ago and it nearly wrecked me. What's this communion, really?" "We'll stand in a circle to signify unity centered on God. We'll say prayers and share bread and wine." "I don't know," said Frank.

"You certainly don't have to know now," said Phil. "And on Sunday, whether or not you have decided, just stand in the circle with everyone else. When the time comes and you feel ready in your heart to receive communion, do. If you don't, you just stand there and decline when the bread and cup are offered. It's your choice. People often decline for any number of reasons. This group will understand whichever way you decide."

The thought rocked Frank to the core. This was supposed to be just a gathering with his friends, not a religious challenge.

* * * * *

Phil visited Nonchalance and talked with her about communion. She chuckled, thanked him, and said that she had long since settled that business. She respected the tradition that he represented, but it was not hers. She would gladly come to the service, would stand in the circle, but would decline to participate in any other way. "It will be good just to be there with my friends. And," she said, "for the party afterward. Don't you guys have some quip about the 'thirst after righteousness'? Would that have anything to do with a little nip after the worship?"

And she also said to Phil, "You know, I have listened to you and these people and all these interpretations of doctrine and laying the template of Christianity over all of life's stuff, and I just don't see where it gets them. It does seem to get them something. For me, my original constitution has served me well out here on Nomanisan Island. I worked it out after I read what Henry Thoreau said about his Walden enterprise, not unlike my Nomanisan enterprise: I went to the island because I wished to live deliberately, to front only the essential facts of life, and see if I could not learn what it had to teach, and not, when I came to die, discover that I had not lived. I did not wish to live what was not life, living is so dear." She looked at Phil. Phil looked at her. They shook hands. Phil went home.

* * * * *

On Sunday morning at Everybody's Inn, Frank's moment of truth closed in on him as he took his place in the circle. In the gathering before communion he had felt the affection that these people expressed for one another. He felt gratitude for their drawing him into their friendship, accepting him just where he was. And wasn't. He admired their acceptance of Nonnie despite her overt rejection of their tradition. Amazing. They respected and celebrated her, nonetheless.

However: Frank was thinking about his hostility about God and his disillusionment about God's treatment of people. These were real issues that were not going away just because he had shed the burdens of wealth and possessions and had come to a new serenity about what was important in his life. Now here he was, his life focusing more and more sharply on this time and place, his new identity forming as each minute brought him closer to the decision. He had never seen the celebration of the communion. He didn't know what was happening as Phil broke the large wafer. But he got the gist, anyhow, of the next words: "The gifts of God for the people of God. Take them in remembrance that Christ died for you, and feed on him in your hearts, by faith, with thanksgiving."

"Gifts of God," "people of God," "feed in your heart," "thanksgiving." That much made sense. He knew his deep hunger and thirst for companionship with God and his friends. He caught on that the bread and the cup offered God's food for his starving spirit. God was feeding everyone equally, bonding them to one another and to God. This he could understand. The rest would have to come later. The plate with the bread appeared in front of him. He lifted his hands and received. The wine appeared. He sipped. Frank came home.

When the circle had heard the closing benediction, they observed a few moments of quiet, then erupted into cheerful greeting, with hugs and handshakes all around. The party went on into the afternoon.

* * * * *

Through a restless night Frank developed some thoughts about his experience of communion. Since eighteen, he had striven against powerlessness, weakness, and sacrifice. Here were people who celebrated them. Since eighteen, he had sought abundance.

Here they gave it away. Since eighteen, every arrangement had been a contract: *quid pro quo*. Now he was learning covenant: nothing pro quo. Since eighteen, he had lived for himself. Here were people who lived for one another. Since eighteen, he had accumulated things and things. Now he had so little, and so much more than before. Since eighteen, he had gotten not mad, but even. Now he got neither. Since eighteen, he had gotten what he paid for. Now he got what he hadn't paid for.

These thoughts brought strength and doubt together. He had seen the people in that circle, he had felt spiritual hunger, he had received bread and wine, and he had sensed a homecoming. But the sheer weirdness of all that talk of incarnation and crucifixion and resurrection, not to mention the Holy Spirit. It all offended common sense.

In that most dark hour before sunrise he got up and dressed, rigged Quest, and set sail. The headstrong craft took Frank back down the river, just the two of them, flogging against a brisk south wind past Mason Neck, past the 301 bridge, past Cobb Island, down toward St. Clement's. All day and into the evening they sailed. Pushing hard, the boat and skipper got to the island before midnight. They anchored east of the island, so Frank could watch the sun hit it from that side. He slept till dawn. It broke cloudy. Nothing particular to see in the dawn's early light. Frank scratched his head and said, for the umpteenth time, "I just don't get it." Quest took him back up the river.

18 The Bottom Line

They all gathered on Easter in Brad and Emily's living room. Hal seemed depressed. He said in a low voice, "On an Easter Sunday like this a quarter century ago, Frank and Sibyl went sailing without me. Sibyl came back dead. Whatever happened to her? Phil, Nonnie, you've answered everything else. But not one useful answer for that. I want to know."

Nonnie spoke up. "I can give you only my opinion, Hal. I think we get this one life, and then we die. We live on in people's memories and what we have done, good and bad. That view protects against speculation and dogmas that promote superstition and institutional agendas. I hope it helps."

Hal looked straight at Nonnie and said, "No, not a bit. Of course her memory lives in my heart. Of course her contribution to this world, our son Frank, lives on. But she had more than that. What? Where now? Conscious? Functioning? In touch with us?"

Emily drew near to Hal and sat on a chair by his. "The grief lives on. The regrets and what-ifs live on. I have no better grip on this than you do, Hal. What grip I once had, celestial bliss or endless perdition, has long since gone into the primitive grave it digs itself. A more adult answer I can't offer."

Phil said, "Hal, I have another answer. If God invites us to communion during our lifetimes, over and over, in steadfast love, why would God not continue to invite us after our mortal days? Why would the nonetheless policy expire when we expire? Anyone care to argue some reason that God, steadfast during our lifetimes, becomes arbitrary when we die?"

Silence. Hal said, "All abstraction, Phil. My engineering mind wants dynamics, practicalities. I'll accept your abstractions as abstractions. They sound okay. But where's Sibyl?"

Phil said, "Well, I suppose we have done all the background we need to take on this speculative matter. So, here goes.

"First, Hal, let's start with what we know. I know that I am a fleshy, bony complex of molecular and cellular structure. I am a mass of matter, arranged as a human body. I also know that I have something in me that animates this body, that provides thinking, speaking, listening, moving. We call it life. I am alive. I further know that bodies stop being alive and that bodies disintegrate. So what's next? Here are several conventional answers.

"Answer one. What's next is nothing. Nothing at all. Death is annihilation. The human, mortal body, all the molecular, cellular structure, is all there is. When the biological life terminates, the human person terminates. When no one remembers you any longer, you no longer exist.

"Answer two. What's next is the pearly gates, where St. Peter calculates your moral worth and decides whether you go into heaven or descend to hell. This popularized view serves us well in jokes.

"Answer three. After death your soul separates from your body and ascends into purgatory, where it waits for the Day of Judgment. When time eventually ends, God will judge whether you have been faithful or wicked, and send you to either heaven or hell for all eternity. The classic portrait of this heaven and hell appears in Dante's fourteenth century poems about hell, purgatory, and heaven.

"The Bible has many passages that you can stitch together to support this view. Parts of the Church employ it, more or less, particularly as a means of behavior control. Your fear of damnation to torture in hell might well modify your behavior.

"All these, however, dismiss God's steadfast love and boundless grace. That's insupportable. So what would be supportable? On what support? I have chosen to support all my positions with the biblical theology we have worked out: God creates, we alienate; nonetheless God continues to invite us to communion.

"This means that God is inviting every person home. I say

again, every person, every race, every creed, every atheist, every criminal. God wants all his treasured people home, back in full communion whence we started. You and I, then, and everybody else, are all journeying back to God.

"Bottom line, that's what we are doing here, why we exist: for present communion with one another and with God. And for ultimate communion with one another and with God. Community. Communion. That's the point of it all.

"I think the Bible shows us that God's steadfast love exerts a gravitational pull Godward toward this communion. Weak enough that your free will can resist it. Strong enough that your free will cannot break its attraction. Resistable but unbreakable.

"How you respond to its invitation has nothing to do with your churchiness or spirituality or intention. Like the mythic Adam and Eve, we are all born into this Godward gravitation of steadfast God-love. From our beginnings we have secure communion with God in our paradise of parent-love.

"But, again like Adam and Eve, something in us causes us to become alienated from God and one another. God nonetheless continues to love us and invite us. As life continues, some of us do feel the gravitational love and do draw closer to God. Others feel no such Godward pull to communion.

"Everyone's mortal body eventually dies. Then what? In the Episcopal prayer book appears this phrase: 'May so and so go from strength to strength in the life of perfect service.' It comes from language in Psalm 84, verse 7, and Colossians 1, verse 10. Also, in the communion service appears a prayer that those who have died may have 'continual growth in [God's] love and service.'

"Taken together, these indicate that when you die, your personhood, the Emily-ness of Emily, the Brad-ness of Brad, continues to exist. How? Beyond this finite time and space. Infinity, eternity, transcendence. We continue on in a resurrectional condition. What's that? Growing Godward.

"Remember, though, that your personhood, even after death, includes your free will. You will be able to resist and refuse. But I think that once we have left all the baggage of mortality, we may be more open to the attraction of God's love.

"So that's what I think goes on after death: continuous growth in God's love and service. God invites us to move toward ultimate communion with God, closeness to God.

"Please remember that I am talking about every human person of whatever religious persuasion and whatever moral condition, now and future and past to the very genesis of humankind. All God's beloved children.

"Again, this viewpoint takes its rationale directly from our biblical theology: God loves all creation, God grieves our alienation, God wants us all back, back close, back around the family table, close and secure.

"But I think God wants us to choose to come back, doesn't want to coerce anyone, command or remand anyone. God won't drag anyone kicking and screaming into the dining room. Nor will God drag anyone kicking and screaming out of the dining room, let alone lock the door. If we wish to resist and reject, we will be at liberty to do that.

"I further think that when you die, you will discover that you could be in full communion with God. You will want to accept the peace, the communion that God offers. You will choose to draw nearer.

"How? All the features of your personhood that have alienated you, all your sinfulness, all your negatives, all your wrongdoing, all will molt like the outgrown shell of a crab, leaving room to grow. All that has separated you from God and others will fall away, leaving you the innocent you were at birth. For God continues always to create, to make all things new. You are now and always will be a work in progress. At the last you will be fulfilled.

"God will transform you into your resurrection body. You will come to the Last Judgment, when you will make your final choice: to accept communion with God. Or to reject God. To accept will be heaven. To reject will be hell."

* * * * *

So. Where's Sibyl?

19 After All

This book is not finished, but I am. I have more in mind, but no more energy to write it.

For example, What, if anything, does God do about our prayers? How, by what physical mechanism does God intervene in the workings of the world? God's fixed laws of nature must operate reliably, inflexibly. Can't disturb those. So I am drawn to the possibilities in quantum physics, such as the Heisenberg uncertainty principle. Looks like some loopholes there, some places where God immanent might fiddle the rigors of natural law in ordinary causality without breaking the reliable laws. But what do I know? Pure speculation. In such matters I suffer that wonderful category known as invincible ignorance. Anyhow, one of these days I'll try to get that concept together.

What about the worrisome fact that creationists are successfully undermining the education of our youngsters in science. Why? Because evidently they think that science, particularly evolution, discredits the Bible, which discredits Christian faith, which leads to atheism, which sanctions immorality. Polls over the past several decades have shown a steady proportion of the American public, between forty and fifty percent, not accepting evolution as an explanation of the origins of humankind. We need scientists to advance medical research, resistance to further global warming, alternative sources of energy, and so forth. Creationists are jeopardizing the teaching of science that will provide those scientists. They are working through local school boards, to influence, for instance, textbook selection and science curriculum standards. Worrisome.

We never found out what Stevie's offence was or why it bothered Brad and Emily so much. I don't know. They never said and I never asked.

I'm sorry I didn't tell you more about Silas and Edna. As you saw, Silas mentored young Frank well, and Edna's information from the Farriers' dining room, channeled through Silas, made Frank's good timing possible. So Frank owed them much. But they made it on their own. Silas was elected CEO of Grant International and Edna went on from heading the county office on affordable housing to become a county supervisor. And would you believe that when Frank went into that communion circle at Everybody's Inn, who should be standing right next to him but Edna and Silas. Their lost cause? Frank never found out and they weren't saying. Some losses stay lost.

Other loose ends, like Nick (a classic loose end) heading for Las Vegas, will have to stay loose, just like in life. And Brad, with his insistent atheism. How authentic do you think that is? He never persuaded me that he had more than an ideological atheism. And Emily. In these two, I see the inherent, invisible unity between science and biblical spirituality. I think they winked at each other when they took such opposing public views.

I never really articulated the comprehensive theology I yearn for. It would stand on a foundation of the holistic biblical theology we got from Phil. This holistic biblical theology would counter the proof-texting biblicism that feeds fundamentalism. My theology would braid scientific and biblical data into a single strand of understanding, each complementing the other and countering the false dichotomy of science versus religion. And that would in turn yield an understanding of providence, how God interacts with us. And that in turn would help us understand what happens when we pray and give us grounds for an adult relationship with God.

So maybe some day I'll go after this comprehensive theology. In the meantime, here is a one-sentence outline: my conviction that God transcendent originated the Big Bang expansion that is creating out of nothing all that is, including this earth in this small cosmic zone where life could emerge to evolve humankind with our capacity to choose and to develop the writings that became our Bible revealing God both transcendent and immanent whose boundless grace-love assures us of our mission to promote the ultimate communion that God will fulfill in the eschaton. Whew.

Shalom.

Printed in the United States
by Baker & Taylor Publisher Services